HIGH STAKES

HIGH STAKES

8 Sure-Bet Stories of Gambling and Crime

Edited by

Robert J. Randisi

A SIGNET BOOK

SIGNET
Published by New American Library, a division of
Penguin Group (USA) Inc., 375 Hudson Street,
New York, New York 10014, U.S.A.
Penguin Books Ltd, 80 Strand,
London WC2R 0RL, England
Penguin Books Australia Ltd, 250 Camberwell Road,
Camberwell, Victoria 3124, Australia
Penguin Books Canada Ltd, 10 Alcorn Avenue,
Toronto, Ontario, Canada M4V 3B2
Penguin Books (N.Z.) Ltd, Cnr Rosedale and Airborne Roads,
Albany, Auckland 1310, New Zealand

Penguin Books Ltd, Registered Offices:
80 Strand, London WC2R 0RL, England

First published by Signet, an imprint of New American Library,
a division of Penguin Group (USA) Inc.

First Printing, September 2003
10 9 8 7 6 5 4 3 2 1

Contents

Introduction

They try to call it "gaming" these days, but we all know that gambling is gambling, don't we? That's what that rush is, whether you're betting a nickel, a dollar, a hundred dollars or—like some of the people in these stories—your life. If you've got nothing to lose, *then* it's a game, but the eight authors in this anthology were not playing games when they wrote these stories.

When I conceived this idea, the authors were invited to write stories that combined crime and gambling. Other than that caveat they were given free reign to write what they wanted. The result was six original stories by some of today's top crime authors and reprints from two of our Grand Masters, all using various versions of "gambling"—including people risking their lives.

Jeff Abbott, Judith Van Gieson and Bob Randisi set their stories in the more traditional gambling venues, such as Las Vegas, Midwest gambling boats and Southwest Indian reservation casinos. Leslie Glass and Elaine Viets went for more hands-on forms of gambling—bingo and dominoes. Jonathon King used a 1920s setting, choosing to place his casino in the Florida Everglades. And finally Larry Block used a private poker game, while Don Westlake's short-short story is set in a Vegas casino, on the Strip.

The idea for this collection came to me when the location for Bouchercon 34 was announced as Las Vegas, in October of 2003. I thought it would be a natural thing to release a gambling anthology in conjunction with the convention, with most or all of the contributors in attendance. Hopefully while you're holding this book in your hands, reading these words, you're also standing in the Dealer's Room at Bouchercon. So pay for this baby and get in line to have it signed before you attend one more panel. But don't worry—if you purchase this book in a bookstore at some later date, there are plenty more conventions coming up.

Bob Randisi
St. Louis, MO
January 2003

Bet on Red

Jeff Abbott

Jeff Abbott is the national bestselling author of three novels of suspense set on the Texas Gulf Coast: the Anthony Award–nominated *A Kiss Gone Bad* (Onyx, 2001), the Edgar Award–nominated *Black Jack Point* (Onyx, 2002), and his latest thriller, *Cut and Run* (Onyx, 2003). Here Jeff switches to a setting that puts him right on the money with the theme of this anthology—Las Vegas!

"I'll make a bet with you," Bobby said. He was bourbon-drunk and he leaned close to Sean's ear to talk over the arpeggios of the piano music, the never-ending chimes of the slot machines, the high roar of gamblers who, just for a moment, were beating the odds.

"I'm listening." Sean thought it was about time to head up to his room, tired of talking to Bobby, just tired, period. Bobby was scaring off all the women with his overeager laughing, raising his glass to passing beauties like an idiot dink. It was a shame, really; this was Bobby's last night to be with a woman and the odds weren't pretty. Sean was supposed to get rid of Bobby tomorrow, take him into the desert outside of Vegas, shoot him, bury him deep in the dry earth and then fly back to Houston with Vic's hundred grand and pretend he hadn't set foot on the Strip recently.

"I bet," Bobby gestured with his near empty glass, "I can nail that pretty little redhead at the end of the bar."

Sean looked. Pretty was an understatement. She was gorgeous, hair that soft color of auburn that made Sean's throat catch, skin flawless as a statue's, dressed tastefully in a little black number that suggested a firm, ripe figure but didn't give away too much of the show. She was sitting alone, not looking at anyone, not trying to make eye contact. Maybe a high-class hooker, maybe not. Maybe just waiting on her boyfriend to finish at the craps table. She was drinking white wine and she cradled the stem of the glass between her palms, like she was keeping a delicate bird from taking wing.

"You aim high," Sean said.

"I got the gun for it," Bobby said.

"And you could impress her with all the cash you got," Sean said. At least temporarily. Sean thought about Vic's money, neat bricks of green he would have to hide in his checked bag tomorrow morning, wishing now he was driving from Vegas to Houston, but what a dreary, endless drive it would have been. He didn't dislike Bobby, didn't like the idea of killing him, but orders were orders and when Vic gave them, you listened.

"Listen, man, that's Vegas for you. The air is thick with constant possibility. You never know which way the ball's gon' drop and then you're broke or rich, all in an instant," Bobby said. "I'm feeling like the ball's dropping my way. She's been looking at me."

"Looking ain't buying," Sean said. "And the keno screen's above your head, buddy."

"But see, that's all Vegas is about. The potential of every single moment." Bobby pulled a wad from his pants pocket, twenties rolled into a thick burrito, and Sean thought, *this is why Vic wants you dead, you dummy.*

"A thousand bucks says I get her," Bobby said.

Sean said nothing. A thousand bucks. Money in his pocket he could take and not feel guilty for taking and keeping after Bobby was dead. If he shot Bobby and then pocketed the money, that would be stealing from Vic, his boss—an unwise move. But if he won the cash from Bobby, then that was fair. Fair as could be. Plus it would be funny to watch Bobby try with the perfect redhead, and hell, if Bobby won, he'd die happier. Harmless. Sean felt an odd tug of friendship for Bobby, soon to die, with his heavy, earnest face flush with life.

"And if you do bed her, what do I have to pay?" Sean said.

"Man," Bobby said, "that happens, I'll have already won."

"That's not a fair bet," Sean said.

"Tell you what: I win," Bobby said, "and you help me straighten out this misunderstanding with Vic. You tell him I've got the deals working just the way he wants."

Vic had sent Bobby to Vegas to shut down his drug operation, sell out the remaining supplies, close the office Bobby ran the deals from three days a week, clean the last hundred grand through the Caymans, pull up stakes and kiss Vegas good-bye. The Feds and the locals were cracking down hard and Vic didn't have enough friends in town to make dealing worthwhile. Bobby didn't want to give up Vegas. And instead of taking three days to wrap up the project Bobby had taken a week, living off Vic's account at the King Midas, apparently doing nothing but drinking and betting and generally not closing shop in any great hurry, keeping the money tied up. And Vic was killing mad.

"That's really between you and Vic," Sean said. "It's your business, Bobby."

"Yeah, but you got his ear more than I do. You could help me a lot. I got the feeling he was a little irritated with me the last time we talked. He doesn't get that it took me longer than I thought it would to collect all the money."

Bobby was fun but dumber than a stump. It didn't matter how long it truly took to gather funds and close shop, it mattered how long Vic gave you to get the work done. Sean finished his beer. Bobby didn't have a chance in hell with the redhead. This was betting with a dead man, and Sean was the house. "Okay," he said. "You're on."

Bobby finished his drink, motioned to the bartender for another. "Observe, grasshopper," he said, moving down toward the redhead.

"Good luck," Sean said, meaning it, being nice, ordering himself another beer for the floor show.

It took about twenty minutes. Sean watched, trying not to watch, Bobby easing onto the stool next to the woman. Sean kept waiting for her to tell Bobby to get lost, to name her price, to ask the bartender to tell Bobby to leave her alone. But instead she gave Bobby a soft, kind smile, talked with him, a little shyly at first, then laughed, let him order her another glass of wine. Once she looked toward Sean, seeing him watching them, maybe having noticed him sitting with Bobby before, knowing he was the friend watching his friend make a move. But she didn't smile at Sean and she looked right back at Bobby, who was now playing it cool, not overeager like he had been the hour before.

They finally got up when she finished her second glass of wine and headed into the acre of casino proper, Bobby giving Sean a knowing wiggle of eyebrow and a subtle thumbs-up with his hand at his side, Sean raising his beer in toast, a little surprised, the redhead never glancing Sean's way.

See you in the morning, Bobby mouthed.

Sean watched them head out into the hubbub of the slot machines and gaming tables, smiling for a minute. Well, it was one sweet way to spend your last night on earth. The angels were on Bobby's side. Sean downed his beer, went out to the roulette table, bet twice on black, watched the ball fall wrong both times, his chips vanish. He didn't really like betting. He remembered that a little too late.

Sean tried Bobby's hotel room early the next morning, about seven, figuring the guy would be sacked out, sleeping late on the last day of his life.

"Yeah?" A woman's voice, sleepy. But polite. A little smoke and purr in her voice. Bobby must have done right by her.

"Is Bobby there?"

"He's in the shower. May I have him call you?" May, not can. The redhead was a nice lady.

"No, thanks, I'll just call him later." Not wanting to leave his name.

"May I tell him who's calling—" she started, but Sean hung up. Got himself showered and dressed, fast, now wanting to get the job done, collect Bobby and the money, kill the poor guy, go home.

Sean called Bobby's room again. No answer, fifteen minutes after he first called. He didn't leave a message on the voice mail system, decided he didn't want to stop by Bobby's room, risk the redhead seeing his face again. Bobby was a breakfast eater, loving the cheap but lavish Vegas buffets, and so Sean headed down to the restaurant. It was crowded with tourist gamblers in vacation clothing, a few bored teenagers, some conventioneering high-tech geeks wearing golf shirts with corporate logos on the pockets.

No Bobby working through a fat omelette, alone or with the redhead. Sean got coffee and a plate of eggs and bacon and sat down in a corner booth, wearing his sunglasses. If Bobby came in, he could excuse himself quickly, tell Bobby to come to his room in an hour, let him enjoy his last meal.

They didn't show. Maybe Bobby'd taken the redhead out for a nicer breakfast than one might find here at the King Midas. Maybe down to Bellagio or Mandalay Bay.

Sean finished his breakfast, checked his cell phone. One message. From Vic.

"Hey, bud," Vic said. "Just calling to see if you're knocking 'em dead in Vegas." That Vic.

His little code was a scream. "Hope you're winning big. Call me when you're back."

A little niggle of panic started in his stomach. Sean ignored it, finished his coffee, kept scanning the crowd for Bobby's blond hair, listening for the boom of his voice. Nothing. Tried Bobby's cell phone. No answer.

Sean waited another thirty minutes, tried Bobby's room again, got nothing. He went up to the room, used the extra key Bobby had given him when he got to Vegas yesterday. Bed a mess, Bobby's clothes still in the closet. The slightest scent of perfume was in the air—the redhead smelled like rose petals and spice. But the bathroom was clean, the shower dry, the towels in maid-hung precision.

He's in the shower. But no one had showered in this room.

"No, no, no," Sean said to himself. "Not after I was a nice guy." He ran from the room, his heart thick in his chest, and headed straight down to the lobby.

Sean drove his rental car down the Strip, then to Sahara Avenue, to the leased office Vic had rented when he and Bobby set up the Vegas operation two months ago, before Vic started feeling pressure from the Feds and decided Vegas made him overextended. The sign on the door read PRIORI CONSULTING, which Vic and Bobby had thought clever, because consulting could mean it was any kind of business, and the legal term sounded respectable and fancy.

Sean had a key and he tried the lock.

The door opened. The office was simple, just a desk and a chair and a laptop computer. A motivational poster on the wall said ACHIEVE, with some dink standing atop a mountain summit at dawn, arms raised in triumph. Like that was supposed to impress Sean or Vic, hard evidence of Bobby's absent work ethic. No Bobby. Sean locked the door behind him, set the deadbolt.

He went straight to the little vault in the back room of the office. Opened it with the combination Vic had given him, not wanting Bobby to know he knew the combo, not wanting to make a big deal about the money.

It was gone. Every last sweet brick of green was gone.

Sean sat in the King Midas bar, peeling the label off his beer in long strips, thinking *this is my skin when Vic gets hold of me.*

Bobby was gone.

Sean felt like control over his own fate had danced right out of his arms, like he was one of those losers who surrendered all to the spinning roulette ball, waiting for it to drop into red or black or a sacred number, every hope in the world wrapped up on how that damned ball fell. Now his generous act was going to screw over his life big time. Maybe the redhead would show back up here, if she were a working girl or a guest. He thought she might be a working girl; not many women came to Vegas alone. Maybe she knew where Bobby had run to. But she had lied about the shower, he believed, Bobby maybe paid her to lie. Give him a head start on his run.

Sean didn't know a soul in Vegas who could help him find Bobby, didn't know any of the street-level dealers Bobby recruited, and he had not known what else to do other than go back to the bar, cancel his flight to Houston and pray he got a lead on Bobby.

He had started to call Vic twice, hung up before finishing the number. Not knowing what he could say, almost laughing because he was afraid, scared in a way he didn't want to admit, trying to imagine the words coming from his mouth: _Bobby wanted to get laid, and it just didn't seem likely, so I let him out of my sight. We had a bet. Sorry._

He switched to vodka martinis and was deep into his second when she came in and sat at the bar.

At first he blinked, not sure it was the same redhead. But it was, this time in leather pants and a white ruffled blouse, simple but stylish.

She looked relaxed and she didn't look over at him. She ordered a glass of pinot grigio.

Sean counted to one hundred, waiting to see if Bobby trailed in behind her. Please, Jesus. But no Bobby. Sean got up from the bar stool, took his martini glass with him, eased next to her. She glanced at him.

"I'm Bobby's friend," he said in a low voice.

"I know. And you're probably a little more shaken," she said, glancing at his martini, "than stirred." Her smile was cool, not shy, not surprised. Expecting to see him, maybe even happy about it.

"Where is he?" Sean asked.

She took a dainty sip of wine. "He's resting. Comfortably."

"Where?" Trying to keep his voice calm.

"Some place you won't find him."

"I can look pretty freaking hard, honey. Tell me where he is. Right now."

She ran a fingernail along the stem of her glass and let a few heavy seconds pass before she answered. "You're not really in a position to make demands."

"Not in a crowded bar."

"Not anywhere," she said. "You need to remember that. I'm not working alone. You're being watched wherever you go."

He was silent for several seconds, thinking *what the hell is this?* "I'll remember," he said.

There was nothing to be gained by threatening her. Play it cool, he decided, play along, and get her alone and then she'd talk. She was enjoying the driver's seat, relishing it a bit too much, and that was a mistake.

"So, this is the deal," the redhead said. "Bobby had a hundred grand in cash on him. You get ten grand, just to tell one little white lie. Tell Vic you took care of Bobby but he had already blown the hundred grand gambling."

"And Vic just believes me?" Sean said.

"We both know," she said, "that yes, Vic will believe you. If you want, we'll get a statement from a couple of blackjack and baccarat dealers that a guy matching Bobby's description blew through a hundred grand in the past week."

"What about the rest of the money?"

"Not your concern. But Bobby walks and gets a new life somewhere else."

"And still has every reason to tell the cops about Vic. And me. No way."

"Sean," she said. "Do you think Bobby would do jail well?"

He surprised them both by laughing. She gave him back a smile, and the intelligence was sharp in her face, she was clearly no dumb bunny–Vegas lay. "Actually, no, Bobby wouldn't do jail well at all. Be dead or someone's punk in five minutes."

"So you and I both know he's not going to run to the police or the FBI and talk about Vic."

"But he might go into WitSec, cut a deal that keeps him out of jail," Sean said.

Her smiled faded. "That's a risk you take. You're not getting close to him," she said. "I've offered you the deal."

"Usually with Vic," he said, "I bring back a finger as proof." This was a lie but he wanted to see her reaction. Vic would think he was a freak if he hauled back a bloodied finger.

"In your carry-on or in your checked luggage?" Not blinking, not afraid at his announcement.

"In a little baggie, actually."

"Messy at security, and I don't believe you."

"Who are you?" he asked.

"You can call me Red."

"I'm impressed with the setup. You in with Bobby from the beginning?"

"I never met him until last night," she said.

"I think that's the first lie you've told me," he said.

"Think what you like," Red said. Her smile went crooked and she took a sip of her white wine. "Tell me. How were you going to spend the bet? The thousand bucks?"

"He told you, huh?"

"Yes." She watched the bartender approach

them and she shook her head. The barkeep went back to the other end of the bar.

"Fishing gear, I guess."

"Fishing gear." She said it like she might say *urine sample*. "I am so flattered that it was my maidenly virtue versus accessorizing your bass boat."

Despite himself, he felt a blush creep up his collar.

Now Red gave him a sly sideways glance. "You want to make a bet with me, Sean?"

"No. I want to conclude our business and never see you again."

"Now you've hurt my feelings," she said with a coy pout.

"I'll bet you heal fast," Sean said.

"Bobby said you were ex-military."

"Yeah, I was a grunt once."

"I've always thought military men had a sense of honor."

"I do," Sean said.

"I have a sense of honor, too. I won't screw you over, you won't screw me and Bobby over. We're all happier. Do we have a deal?"

"Don't kid yourself that I want to cut a deal with you, honey. What if I say no?"

"Then you'll be killed," Red said. "How does that sound?"

He watched her face, chewed the last olive in his martini, swallowed the small puddle of vodka at the glass's bottom. Watched her face for a hint of bluff and didn't see any. "Bobby sure got smart since he got to town."

"This town forces you to be smarter, Sean," she said, and now she smiled at him and it seemed genuine, like they hadn't discussed big money and death.

"It hasn't worked on me yet," Sean said.

"You're plenty smart, hon," Red said. "So agree to this. Come to the Misty Moor Bar—off the Strip, near the Convention Center—in two hours. Alone and unarmed. Break either rule and you're dead. You'll get your money then. You will be expected to leave Vegas immediately; we'll even escort you to the airport."

She swung her legs off the bar stool, pulled a ten from her purse.

"I'll buy your wine," Sean said. "You can buy my drink at the other bar."

She tucked the bill back inside. "Thanks. I'll see you then," she said. "And, Sean?"

"What?"

"It's nothing personal. Bobby likes you. So do I."

Red turned and walked out, and he debated whether he should follow her. He counted to twenty, left money on the counter, got up from the bar stool, headed out and hung back in the casino's crowd.

She never looked back to see if he trailed her.

But if she wasn't working alone, as she said, then her partners might be watching him this very moment. He stayed back as far as he dared, weaving through the slot machiners hooting at their triple cherries, past a rail-thin lady carrying a bucket of coins with all the care she would give the Holy Grail, past honeymooners nuzzling in the lobby. She headed past the bell attendants dressed like ancient Greeks. There was no taxi line at the moment and she quickly ducked into a cab with a promo for a wireless phone service mounted on the trunk, a monkey wearing eyeglasses talking on a cellular.

As soon as her cab pulled out of the circular driveway he grabbed a taxi, told the Nigerian driver to head down the Strip and said, "See that cab up ahead? With the monkey talking on the phone? Follow it, please."

"Excuse?"

"The ad on the back. See?" She was five cars ahead of them, her driver changing lanes, and Sean could taste his own panic in his mouth, sour and coppery. "Jesus, keep up, don't lose them, but don't get too close."

"Ah," the driver said. "No trouble is wanted."

"That's my girlfriend," he said, "and I think she's dumping me to go back to her husband. I don't want trouble, I just want to know, 'cause if she's leaving me, I'm just gonna go back to my wife."

The Nigerian made a low noise in his throat that sounded like "Americans" but said nothing more.

Screw this meeting on her turf. He wasn't about to risk Vic's rage for a measly ten grand. Let her take him straight to Bobby. He would end their little game tonight, and then get the hell out of town.

The cab took her to a small house, in an older, quiet residential area distant from all the neon and glam. Not a well-to-do neighborhood but not too scruffy. He told the driver to let him off at the corner where her cab had turned, and shoved fifty at the Nigerian, who babbled thanks and revved off. Sean sprinted away from the corner, out of her line of sight. He couldn't see Red but her cab was pulling away from a house nine homes down from where he was, marked with a decorative covered wagon mailbox.

This was, he decided, a good hideout for Bobby. Quiet neighborhood, probably not a lot of crime, older folks who kept an eye on each other. Maybe it was the woman's house, although she looked like she came from money. Or had money. The easy, unafraid confidence she had with him, the nice clothes she'd worn both nights.

He felt a lava-heat anger with Bobby; oddly,

he didn't wish Red ill at the moment and his re-action surprised himself. He liked her; Vic would have liked her too, but she had chosen the wrong side. She was the kind of girl he'd like to have taken back to Houston, taken out to dinner with Vic. She would have made Sean look good, would have had fun with him. Stupid Bobby, getting himself and this cool girl killed.

Sean headed for the next street, which ran parallel to the street she'd stopped on. In case she'd seen the cab, gotten suspicious. If she'd seen him, she and Bobby would run and that might be the end of the money and of Sean.

He walked down a little street called Pelican Way—where the hell were there pelicans in Nevada? he wondered—counting houses, just giving her and Bobby time to relax, letting them start to get ready for meeting him at the bar. He counted nine houses, stopped in front of one. Brick, a one-car carport, wind chimes hanging by the front door, the trim and shutters needing a fresh coat of paint.

This ranch-style should be directly behind Red's house. He changed his plan. The house was dark, entirely so, no cars in the small drive-way, old oil leaks marring the carport's concrete. The house next door was dark, too, although the house on the other side had a single light gleaming on its porch. He turned like he belonged here and walked, casually, straight up the driveway. He went through the carport, paused at the fence, listened for the rasp of dog breath and then opened the gate and went inside.

The backyard was empty except for a swingset, an old barbecue, dusty patio furniture in need of a wash. Sean went to the fence and tiptoed onto the rail, peering into Red's backyard. Three lights on in the house. A kitchen with an old style bay window. Then he saw Red talking on the phone, moving from the kitchen table to the counter, sipping from a water bottle, moving back again. He ducked back down under the fence. Waited a minute. Looked again.

Now the kitchen was empty. He watched, counted to two hundred. Didn't see movement in the house. Counted to two hundred again, looked. All appeared quiet.

No guards, no dogs. The thought that Red must be part of a rival drug ring in town who'd convinced Bobby to switch sides occurred to him, but then he thought not. She didn't seem the gang type. Maybe she really was just working with him, no one else, a heist by her and Bobby. He hoped. It would make his work easier.

Sean went over the fence, dropped down, sprinted for the patio. He had a Glock under his jacket and as he ran he pulled it free. He got to the patio, waited against the door. Listened to the soft buzz of the TV. Sounded like an old John

Wayne movie, the distinctive rise and fall of the Duke saying, "Hell, yes, I'm back in town."

Then he heard Red's voice, gentle: "I'll be back in a little while, all right? Enjoy the movie." No answer from whoever she was talking to.

Sean moved away from the door. He heard a door open to his right, into the one-car garage. Light footsteps, just one person, heels, a woman's step. Red, alone. Then a car starting, pulling out of the driveway, headlights flickering on at the last moment. She had a car but had taken a taxi to King Midas so he couldn't follow her to a parked car in the lot. Smart girl. Sean stayed still, counted to one hundred. He went around to the carport, tried the door to the house. Locked.

He popped the glass pane in the door, and it tinkled, surely loud enough for Bobby to hear inside the house. So he worked quickly, reaching inside, fingers fumbling to unlock the door.

There was no deadbolt. Instead, there was another key lock. Bobby was locked in from both sides. Weird. He leveled his pistol through the broken glass, waiting for Bobby to barrel out at the sound of the break-in, but there was no sound in the darkened house except the melodramatic score of the Western, faint as a whisper.

Sean waited ten seconds, a tremble of panic thumping his guts, and decided standing there waiting for Bobby to charge the door wasn't bright. He went back to the patio and kicked in the glass door. Loud shattering noise. Two houses down a dog barked, sharp and hard, twice; then quiet. Sean counted to twenty. Nothing. No concerned neighbors popping a head over the fence.

Sean flicked open the door handle, slid the door open.

The room was a sunken den and the kitchen was to his right. A hallway went off at a left angle. He waited, his gun leveled at the opening, and waited some more. He could hear the sound of horses riding hard and stopping, of John Wayne mouthing a good-natured threat, of a polite man answering with an oozy official tone.

Sean inched down the hallway, the gun out like he'd learned in his days in the army. A feeble spill of light—from a television—came from a room at the end of the hall. He moved toward it, calming his breathing, listening for the sound of Bobby moving, and finally Sean charged fast into the room, going through the door, covering the room with his gun.

Bobby was there. Both hands cuffed to a bed, gagged with a cloth jammed in his mouth and duct tape masking his mouth, ribboning into his hair. One of his eyes was bruised. He was shirtless, dressed only in the khakis from last night with a wet circle of stain on the front, and he smelled like he needed a shower. A pile of pillows kept his head propped up. A little television with a VCR stood on a scruffy bureau, the John Wayne movie playing.

Sean stared for a moment, then shook his head.

Bobby groaned, made pleading noises behind the gag. Sean muted the TV, left the tape running, John Wayne swaggering across a saloon.

"Are you going to scream if I take this off?" Sean asked. "I mean, Vegas is just full of possibilities, isn't it, Bobby? So you said."

Bobby shook his head.

Sean pulled the tape and gag from Bobby's head, not worrying about the threads of hair that ripped free with the industrial tape, and Bobby said, "Oh, thank God, man. Thank God, Sean. I knew you'd find me. Get me the hell out of here."

Sean sat down on the edge of the little bed. "Tell me what's happened." Calm. Curious to hear what the story was, because this tied-up-and-bound gig was not what he expected.

"That bitch, man, she's crazy. Drugged me and tied my ass up. Christ, she's *nuts*. Untie me, man."

"Just a minute," Sean said. "You're not in with her?"

"In with her?" Bobby stared. He jerked at the handcuffs. "Do I look like it?"

"I went to your office looking for your sorry ass," Sean said. "And all of Vic's money is missing. The whole hundred grand."

Bobby's lips—chapped and blistered from the tape—turned into a frown. "Holy shit. She must've taken it."

"She was in your hotel room when I called this morning."

"Shit, man, she slipped something into my drink and knocked my ass out. I woke up here. She must've snuck me out of the hotel somehow. She's got inside help. She probably took all my keys, took the money. Unhook me, Sean. Jesus, let's get the hell out of here." An edge in his voice; Sean thought he was about to cry.

"God, you're dumb. You are so unrelentingly dumb. Did she bring the money here?"

"I don't know, I don't know—just untie me, please, before she gets back here!"

"No hurry." Sean checked his watch. "Because she's heading off to meet me at a bar. She's negotiating on your behalf, buddy, for me to tell Vic that you're dead and for you to keep all his money."

Bobby struggled against the shackles, pulling his head up from the pillows. "That's a goddamned lie. I'm not trying to steal Vic's money! She's set you up. Listen, untie me; we'll wait for her to come back and then we'll make her tell us who she's working for."

"You never saw her before?"

"No, man, I swear it. *Swear it!*"

"But she knows your business. She knows about you working for Vic. She knows my name. She knows there was a safe in the office and she got the combo. You must've seen her before."

"No, I swear."

"Then you must've blabbed to somebody, and that's who she's working with."

"No, never, never," Bobby said, but his voice dropped a notch, spurred by a little jiggle of memory, a thought of a mistake made and now wished away.

"Right, Bobby. Never would you make a mistake. You wear my ass out just listening to you."

"Listen, Sean, she's the bad guy, not me. We can get the money back. Together."

Sean said nothing for a moment, thinking it out, feeling very tired and then wired, all at once. He stood up. Went and searched the house carefully and efficiently. There was scant furniture in the house; he decided it was a rental.

"Sean?" Bobby called quietly. "Sean?"

"Just a minute. Hush," Sean said. No sign of the money anywhere. It wasn't here. He went back to the bedroom, Bobby watching him with eyes glassy with sick fear.

"Sean, you're my friend; Vic's my friend; you

know I had nothing to do with this girl's scheme."

"You know, I believe you, Bobby," Sean said. "Had to chase the wrong girl, didn't you?" He nearly laughed. He had made his decision.

"Yeah, I guess," Bobby said.

"Did you get her?" Sean asked, wondering what he'd say.

"No," Bobby said after a moment.

"Then I guess I win the bet."

"Well, that was a bad bet to make," Bobby said.

"That's real true." Sean stood up, turned up John Wayne. Real loud.

Sean had thought the "Misty Moore" was maybe a bar named after the owner, some chick named Misty, but instead it was Moor without the *e* on the end, and when he went inside he noticed a silver thistle above the bar and the waitresses wore tams on their heads and snug little kilts across their asses and the wallpaper was plaid. He spotted Red sitting in a very private back corner booth, drinking her white wine. The bar was not terribly crowded, a dozen conventioneers watching a basketball game on the big screen, a few locals. He slid into the booth, sitting next to her, not across from her.

"You take the low road," he said, "and I'll take the high road."

"Cute. Scotland was one of the few cultures not raided by Vegas," Red said. She was very calm. "Then *Braveheart* came out and they opened up this place. If you get drunk, they'll paint your face blue."

A waitress approached them and asked Sean what he would drink. "Scotch," he said. "Obviously."

"You're a few minutes late," Red said when the waitress walked off. "Fortunately I'm patient and forgiving."

"More reason to admire you," he said. "Let's get to it."

"I've got your ten thousand," she said. "You still agreeing to lie to Vic, let Bobby walk?"

"Actually, the deal has changed, Red." He kept his voice low and the waitress returned with his Scotch, set it down in front of him, walked off back to the bar.

Red was very still. "Changed?"

"You have the hundred grand. You also have a dead man in your house. You know, your house at 118 Falcon Street. Where you had the John Wayne movie marathon playing." He saw the shift in her face, saw she believed him now. "So, baby, I can call the police, from that phone right over there in the corner, and I figure they can be at your house faster than you or anybody else can be dragging Bobby's body out to your car. You'll have a lot of questions to answer."

"So will you," she said, staying calm.

"No, I won't. Because I sure don't know you, and you can't prove that I know you. Or that I knew Bobby."

"You would have been seen with him at the hotel."

"Maybe. Maybe those folks don't talk after Vic calls his friends at the casino. But Bobby-boy's dead in your house."

"I haven't shot a gun anytime recently. They have chemical tests . . ."

"I wouldn't waste a good bullet on Bobby. Smothered with a pillow, sweetheart," Sean said. "How hard they got to look for a new suspect?"

Red took a microscopic sip of her wine. She set the glass down carefully. "So. What now?"

"Who else here's with you?" he asked.

"No one."

"You had help in getting Bobby out of the King Midas. So don't lie to me. It makes me want to call 911." He smiled at her, touched her hand gently. "You're no longer running the show, sweetness."

She let two beats pass. "The guy in the windbreaker at the bar. He's my partner." Sean allowed himself a very quick glance. The guy was watching them, not threatening, but worried, and he glanced into his beer right when Sean looked at him. The guy was big but had a soft-

ness to his hands and his mouth, had a nervous-
ness to him that made Sean feel confident.

"How'd you find out about Bobby and the
money?" Sean asked.

She gestured to the waitress for another glass
of wine, and he knew then she would tell him,
that he had her. "My partner works for an office
equipment leasing company. He delivered
Bobby's office equipment when Bobby got
started. Late in the day, he and Bobby got to
talking. Ended up going out for a beer. Bobby
doesn't like to be alone, ever, and here he was
new in a big town where he didn't know anybody. They got to be drinking buddies and Bobby'd give my partner a little coke now and then
when he came to town. One night Bobby drank
too much, talked plenty. The safe combo—Jesus,
Bobby stuck the numbers on a sticky note in his
desk drawer. Not the brightest star in the sky."

"And you were the handy redhead."

"It's not natural," Red said. "I spent $250 on
this hair color at a really uppity salon on the
Strip after Bobby told my friend he dug redheads."

"Looks good," Sean said.

"Thank you," she said.

Sean looked back at the bar and now her partner kept his stare on Sean. "Your friend appears
to be a little nervous," he said. "Are we going to
have a problem?"

"No."

"He more than a friend?"

"My brother."

"Oh, please."

"No, really, he is. No joke."

"I love a family that works together," Sean said. "Okay, wave Bubba over here."

She did and at first the brother, uncool, acted like he didn't see her. But then she stood up and said, "Garry, come here, please," clear as a bell and Garry got up and came and sat across from Sean and Red. His mouth was thin. Scared, in over his head.

Sean didn't smile, didn't say hello or offer his hand. "So, the two of you thought you could screw me over."

"Not you," Red said, "Bobby and Vic. Jesus, you act like it was personal." Her smile warmed a little. "I told you it wasn't."

"Doesn't matter," Sean said. "You got a dead guy in your house. What I don't have is what I came here for, Vic's money. Now. I give you guys credit; the scheme was clever. You get rid of Bobby, get the money, and make Vic think that Bobby's on the run so he never, ever comes hunting for you."

"Thank you," Red said.

"You're welcome," Sean said. "I want that money here on this table in ten minutes or I'm calling the police and telling them that there's a

funny smell coming from y'all's guest bedroom."

Garry went white as salt. Red took a calm sip
of her wine.

"And if we don't cooperate, you get nothing,"
she said. "You get screwed over just as bad as
us, because Vic'll kill you, won't he?"

"Of course not," Sean said.

"Really? You'll have failed in your errand and
he's not gonna take it lightly," Red said. "Bobby
told me all about him, and we did some check-
ing on him. People piss themselves when Vic
comes into a room."

"Maybe Bobby did. He's easily impressed,"
Sean said, and for the first time Red laughed.

"He was impressed with you, Sean. He liked
you. Truly."

Sean felt a pang of regret, wanted to close his
eyes, but instead put a hard stare on his face.
"Don't tell me that; you'll make me feel bad."

"I'll make you feel worse," Red said. "If you
send us to jail, you go home empty-handed.
You'll never get your money because we'll give
it to the cops, cut a deal to tell all we know about
you and Vic and Bobby, and you're just as dead
as we are. So call 911, Sean. We'll sit here and
wait."

"For God's sakes . . ." Garry said.

"Hush, now," Red said. "Sean's thinking. He
needs his quiet time."

They had him by the throat just as surely as he had them. Standoff.

"So there's no way out for any of us," Red said, "unless we work together. And unless you're willing to get out from under Vic's thumb."

"I'm not under his thumb," Sean said.

"There's two types of people in this world," Red said. "Bosses and errand boys. Bobby, at least during his time in Vegas, he got to be a boss. But you're always gonna be Vic's errand boy, aren't you? He could've kept his business running in Vegas, given it to you, let you take the risk. And the reward." She leaned forward and he could smell the rose perfume he'd smelled in Bobby's hotel room with its lie-dry shower, the soft scent of wine on her breath. "Are you always going to be an errand boy, Sean?"

He said nothing, watching her.

"I mean, say Vic was out of the picture, you could take over in Vegas. There's a whole infrastructure of dealers and customers in place, ready for someone smarter than Bobby to step in. Make more money than an errand boy ever would. I could help you, Sean. We could get rid of Vic. Together. It beats sending each other to prison." And she gave him a wry grin.

"I can't just kill Vic. The rest of his organiza-

tion would come after me like an army." That
was all of ten guys, but it was enough.

"Not if something happened to him here.
Away from them, where they couldn't know exactly what had happened. Maybe the same trouble that happened to Bobby. A rival gang, let's
say. Vic dies, you take over the operation before
the other gang can, you're a hero. End of story."

"What," Sean said, "are you suggesting?"
Feeling another rush of decision, of possibility,
imagining a roulette ball spinning in her smile.

"Tell me," Red said, "does Vic like redheads?"

The King Midas bar, two nights later, was qui-
eter than the first time Sean had been in here
with Bobby, a different bartender, tonight a
black woman with a soft Jamaican accent. Vic
watched her walk to the other side of the bar.
They were at a back table but with a good view
of the curved teak of the bar.

"These Caribes," Vic said. "They're everywhere. If you grew up on an island, why would
you want to move to a goddamned desert?" He
coughed once, sipped hard at his vodka and
tonic. "It's pissing me off."

"Change of pace." Sean cleared his throat.
"I'm sorry this has turned into a hassle, but I'm
confident we can catch the bastards that kid-
napped Bobby."

"You got a lead on these assholes?" Vic took another tense swallow of vodka.

"Asians from Los Angeles, moving east," Sean said. "That's the word on the street." The lie was easy now, practiced in his mind, and it made sense.

Vic frowned. "Let 'em kill Bobby for all I care. Why should I meet with them?"

"Listen, he talks before he dies, and they've got the information to bring you down," Sean said. "They can feed it to informants, cut a deal to trade you to the cops on a platter if any of their chiefs get caught. You need Bobby back in one piece. Plus, they're being too clever, wanting to meet, wanting more money. Greed is stupid in this case. We'll kill them."

"Christ," Vic said. "You're sure this ain't a trap they're setting?"

"I'm sure," Sean said, and he saw Red walk in. Same little black dress as before but now her hair was rich coffee brown, bobbed short, like Sean knew Vic liked. "They're not that smart."

"I want them dead when we're done, you hear me?"

"I hear you," Sean said. "Listen, try to relax. This is Vegas. Have some fun. We can't do anything until the meeting tomorrow, man. Chill out. You want to go see a show?"

Vic said, "Jesus, no, sitting in a chair for two hours would drive me nuts." He finished his vodka, ordered another. Sean waited, giving him time, not wanting to force it. Finally Vic saw her.

"Check out the sweet treat at the bar," Vic said.

"Which?"

"Five stools from the right. The tasty brunette."

"She's out of your league, Vic, a little too pretty." Pushing Vic's button.

Vic raised an eyebrow but wasn't mad. Smiling at the challenge. "This from the little league."

"I'm just saying, she looks like she's happy alone," Sean said. "She wouldn't want to talk to some guy who's all stressed about his business. Not thinking about having a good time."

"Hey, I want her, I can get her," Vic said.

Sean smiled. "You think so, Vic? How about a little bet?"

Let's Get Lost
A Matt Scudder Story

Lawrence Block

Let's face it, by now Larry Block has probably used every setting or device that exists in the mystery genre—and is even now coming up with something new. His most recent novel was the stand-alone bestseller *Small Town* (Morrow, 2003). Here Larry offers us a wonderful reprint that goes back to Matthew Scudder's drinking days, when he was still a cop—a darker Scudder than readers have seen in recent years. The game here is a private poker game, but the gamble is murder.

When the phone call came I was parked in front of the television set in the front room, nursing a glass of bourbon and watching the Yankees. It's funny what you remember and what you don't. I remember that Thurman Munson had just hit a long foul that missed being a home run by no more than a foot, but I don't remember who they were playing, or even what kind of a season they had that year.

I remember that the bourbon was J. W. Dant, and that I was drinking it on the rocks, but of course I would remember that. I always remembered what I was drinking, though I didn't always remember why.

The boys had stayed up to watch the opening innings with me, but tomorrow was a school day, and Anita took them upstairs and tucked them in while I freshened my drink and sat down again. The ice was mostly melted by the time Munson hit his long foul, and I was still shaking my head at that when the phone rang. I let it ring, and Anita answered it and came in to tell me it was for me. Somebody's secretary, she said.

I picked up the phone, and a woman's voice, crisply professional, said, "Mr. Scudder, I'm calling for Mr. Alan Herdig of Herdig and Crowell."

"I see," I said, and listened while she elaborated, and estimated just how much time it would take me to get to their offices. I hung up and made a face.

"You have to go in?"

I nodded. "It's about time we had a break in this one," I said. "I don't expect to get much sleep tonight, and I've got a court appearance tomorrow morning."

"I'll get you a clean shirt. Sit down. You've got time to finish your drink, don't you?"

I always had time for that.

Years ago, this was. Nixon was president, a couple of years into his first term. I was a detective with the NYPD, attached to the Sixth Precinct in Greenwich Village. I had a house on Long Island with two cars in the garage, a Ford wagon for Anita and a beat-up Plymouth Valiant for me.

Traffic was light on the LIE, and I didn't pay much attention to the speed limit. I didn't know many cops who did. Nobody ever ticketed a brother officer. I made good time, and it must have been somewhere around a quarter to ten when I left the car at a bus stop on First Avenue. I had a card on the dashboard that would keep me safe from tickets and tow trucks.

The best thing about enforcing the laws is that you don't have to pay a lot of attention to them yourself.

Her doorman rang upstairs to announce me, and she met me at the door with a drink. I don't remember what she was wearing, but I'm sure she looked good in it. She always did.

She said, "I would never call you at home. But it's business."

"Yours or mine?"

"Maybe both. I got a call from a client. A Madison Avenue guy, maybe an agency vice president. Suits from Tripler's, season tickets for the Rangers, house in Connecticut."

"And?"

"And didn't I say something about knowing a cop? Because he and some friends were having a friendly card game and something happened to one of them."

"Something happened? Something happens to a friend of yours, you take him to a hospital. Or was it too late for that?"

"He didn't say, but that's what I heard. It sounds to me as though somebody had an accident and they need somebody to make it disappear."

"And you thought of me."

"Well," she said.

She'd thought of me before, in a similar connection. Another client of hers, a Wall Street warrior, had had a heart attack in her bed one afternoon. Most men will tell you that's how they want to go, and perhaps it's as good a way as any, but it's not all that convenient for the people who have to clean up after them, especially when the bed in question belongs to some working girl.

When the equivalent happens in the heroin trade, it's good PR. One junkie checks out with an overdose and the first thing all his buddies want to know is where did he get the stuff and how can they cop some themselves. Because, hey, it must be good, right? A hooker, on the other hand, has less to gain from being listed as cause of death. And I suppose she felt a professional responsibility, if you want to call it that, to spare the guy and his family embarrassment. So I made him disappear and left him fully dressed in an alley down in the financial district. I called it in anonymously and went back to her apartment to claim my reward.

"I've got the address," she said now. "Do you want to have a look? Or should I tell them I couldn't reach you?"

I kissed her, and we clung to each other for a long moment. When I came up for air I said, "It'd be a lie."

"I beg your pardon?"

"Telling them you couldn't reach me. You can always reach me."

"You're a sweetie."

"You better give me that address," I said.

I retrieved my car from the bus stop and left it in another one a dozen or so blocks uptown. The address I was looking for was a brownstone in the East Sixties. A shop with handbags and briefcases in the window occupied the storefront, flanked by a travel agent and a men's clothier. There were four doorbells in the vestibule, and I rang the third one and heard the intercom activated but didn't hear anyone say anything. I was reaching to ring a second time when the buzzer sounded. I pushed the door open and walked up three flights of carpeted stairs.

Out of habit, I stood to the side when I knocked. I didn't really expect a bullet, and what came through the door was a voice, pitched low, asking who was there.

"Police," I said. "I understand you've got a situation here."

There was a pause. Then a voice—maybe the

same one, maybe not—said, "I don't understand. Has there been a complaint, Officer?"

They wanted a cop, but not just any cop. "My
name's Scudder," I said. "Elaine Mardell said
you could use some help."

The lock turned and the door opened. Two
men were standing there, dressed for the office
in dark suits and white shirts and ties. I looked
past them and saw two more men, one in a suit,
the other in gray slacks and a blue blazer. They
looked to be in their early to mid forties, which
made them ten to fifteen years older than me.

I was what, thirty-two that year? Something
like that.

"Come on in," one of them said. "Careful."

I didn't know what I was supposed to be careful of but found out when I gave the door a
shove and it stopped after a few inches. There
was a body on the floor, a man, curled on his
side. One arm was flung up over his head, the
other bent at his side, the hand inches from the
handle of the knife. It was an easy-open stiletto
and it was buried hilt-deep in his chest.

I pushed the door shut and knelt down for a
close look at him. I heard the bolt turn as one of
them locked the door.

The dead man was around their age and had
been similarly dressed until he took off his suit
jacket and loosened his tie. His hair was a little
longer than theirs, perhaps because he was los-

ing hair on the crown and wanted to conceal the bald spot. Everyone tries that, and it never works.

I didn't feel for a pulse. A touch of his forehead established that he was too cold to have one. And I hadn't really needed to touch him to know that he was dead. Hell, I knew that much before I parked the car.

Still, I took some time looking him over. Without looking up I asked what had happened. There was a pause while they decided who would reply, and then the same man who'd questioned me through the closed door said, "We don't really know."

"You came home and found him here?"

"Hardly that. We were playing a few hands of poker, the five of us. Then the doorbell rang and Phil went to see who it was."

I nodded at the dead man. "That's Phil there?"

Someone said it was. "He'd folded already," the man in the blazer added.

"And the rest of you fellows were still in the middle of a hand."

"That's right."

"So he—Phil?"

"Yes, Phil."

"Phil went to the door while you finished the hand."

"Yes."

"And?"

"And we didn't really see what happened," one of the suits said.

"We were in the middle of a hand," another explained, "and you can't really see much from where we were sitting."

"At the card table," I said.

"That's right."

The table was set up at the far end of the living room. It was a poker table, with a green baize top and wells for chips and glasses. I walked over and looked at it.

"Seats eight," I said.

"Yes."

"But there were only the five of you. Or were there other players as well?"

"No, just the five of us."

"The four of you and Phil."

"Yes."

"And Phil was clear across the room answering the door, and one or two of you would have had your backs to it, and all four of you would have been more interested in the way the hand was going than who was at the door." They nodded along, pleased at my ability to grasp all this. "But you must have heard something that made you look up."

"Yes," the blazer said. "Phil cried out."

"What did he say?"

"'No!' or 'Stop!' or something like that. That

got our attention, and we got out of our chairs and looked over there, but I don't think any of us got a look at the guy."

"The guy who . . ."

"Stabbed Phil."

"He must have been out the door before you had a chance to look at him."

"Yes."

"And pulled the door shut after him."

"Or Phil pushed it shut while he was falling."

I said, "Stuck out a hand to break his fall . . ."

"Right."

"And the door swung shut, and he went right on falling."

"Right."

I retraced my steps to the spot where the body lay. It was a nice apartment, I noted, spacious and comfortably furnished. It felt like a bachelor's full-time residence, not a married commuter's pied-à-terre. There were books on the bookshelves, framed prints on the walls, logs in the fireplace. Opposite the fireplace, a two-by-three throw rug looked out of place atop a large Oriental carpet. I had a hunch I knew what it was doing there.

But I walked past it and knelt down next to the corpse. "Stabbed in the heart," I noted. "Death must have been instantaneous, or the next thing to it. I don't suppose he had any last words."

"No."

"He crumpled up and hit the floor and never moved."

"That's right."

I got to my feet. "Must have been a shock."

"A terrible shock."

"How come you didn't call it in?"

"Call it in?"

"Call the police," I said. "Or an ambulance, get him to a hospital."

"A hospital couldn't do him any good," the blazer said. "I mean, you could tell he was dead."

"No pulse, no breathing."

"Right."

"Still, you must have known you're supposed to call the cops when something like this happens."

"Yes, of course."

"But you didn't."

They looked at each other. It might have been interesting to see what they came up with, but I made it easy for them.

"You must have been scared," I said.

"Well, of course."

"Guy goes to answer the door and the next thing you know he's dead on the floor. That's got to be an upsetting experience, especially taking into account that you don't know who killed him or why. Or do you have an idea?"

They didn't.

"I don't suppose this is Phil's apartment."

"No."

Of course not. If it was, they'd have long since gone their separate ways.

"Must be yours," I told the blazer, and enjoyed it when his eyes widened. He allowed that it was and asked how I knew. I didn't tell him he was the one man in the room without a wedding ring, or that I figured he'd changed from a business suit to slightly more casual clothes on his return home, while the others were still wearing what they'd worn to the office that morning. I just muttered something about policemen developing certain instincts and let him think I was a genius.

I asked if any of them had known Phil very well and wasn't surprised to learn that they hadn't. He was a friend of a friend of a friend, someone said, and did something on Wall Street.

"So he wasn't a regular at the table."

"No."

"This wasn't his first time, was it?"

"His second," somebody said.

"First time was last week?"

"No, two weeks ago. He didn't play last week."

"Two weeks ago. How'd he do?"

Elaborate shrugs. The consensus seemed to be

that he might have won a few dollars, but nobody had paid much attention.

"And this evening?"

"I think he was about even. If he was ahead it couldn't have been more than a few dollars."

"What kind of stakes do you play for?"

"It's a friendly game. One-two-five in stud games. In draw it's two dollars before the draw, five after."

"So you can win or lose what, a couple of hundred?"

"That would be a big loss."

"Or a big win," I said.

"Well, yes. Either way."

I knelt down next to the corpse and patted him down. Cards in his wallet identified him as Philip I. Ryman, with an address in Teaneck.

"Lived in Jersey," I said. "And you say he worked on Wall Street?"

"Somewhere downtown."

I picked up his left hand. His watch was Rolex, and I suppose it must have been a real one; this was before the profusion of fakes. He had what looked like a wedding band on the appropriate finger, but I saw that it was in fact a large silver or white-gold ring that had gotten turned around, so that the large part was on the palm side of his hand. It looked like an unfinished signet ring, waiting for an initial to be carved into its gleaming surface.

I straightened up. "Well," I said, "I'd say it's a good thing you called me."

"There are a couple of problems," I told them. "A couple of things that could pop up like a red flag for a responding officer or a medical examiner."

"Like . . ."

"Like the knife," I said. "Phil opened the door and the killer stabbed him once and left, was out the door and down the stairs before the body hit the carpet."

"Maybe not that fast," one of them said, "but it was pretty quick. Before we knew what had happened, certainly."

"I appreciate that," I said, "but the thing is it's an unusual MO. The killer didn't take time to make sure his victim was dead, and you can't take that for granted when you stick a knife in someone. And he left the knife in the wound."

"He wouldn't do that?"

"Well, it might be traced to him. All he has to do to avoid that chance is take it away with him. Besides, it's a weapon. Suppose someone comes chasing after him? He might need that knife again."

"Maybe he panicked."

"Maybe he did," I agreed. "There's another thing, and a medical examiner would notice this if a reporting officer didn't. The body's been moved."

Interesting the way their eyes jumped all over the place. They looked at each other, they looked at me, they looked at Phil on the floor.

"Blood pools in a corpse," I said. "Lividity's the word they use for it. It looks to me as though Phil fell forward and wound up face downward. He probably fell against the door as it was closing, and slid down and wound up on his face. So you couldn't get the door open, and you needed to, so eventually you moved him."

Eyes darted. The host, the one in the blazer, said, "We knew you'd have to come in."

"Right."

"And we couldn't have him lying against the door."

"Of course not," I agreed. "But all of that's going to be hard to explain. You didn't call the cops right away, and you did move the body. They'll have some questions for you."

"Maybe you could give us an idea what questions to expect."

"I might be able to do better than that," I said. "It's irregular, and I probably shouldn't, but I'm going to suggest an action we can take."

"Oh?"

"I'm going to suggest we stage something," I said. "As it stands, Phil was stabbed to death by an unknown person who escaped without anybody getting a look at him. He may never turn up, and if he doesn't, the cops are going to look hard at the four of you."

"Jesus," somebody said.

"It would be a lot easier on everybody," I said, "if Phil's death was an accident."

"An accident?"

"I don't know if Phil has a sheet or not," I said. "He looks vaguely familiar to me, but lots of people do. He's got a gambler's face, even in death, the kind of face you expect to see in an OTB parlor. He may have worked on Wall Street, it's possible, because cheating at cards isn't necessarily a full-time job."

"Cheating at cards?"

"That would be my guess. His ring's a mirror; turned around, it gives him a peek at what's coming off the bottom of the deck. It's just one way to cheat, and he probably had thirty or forty others. You think of this as a social event, a once-a-week friendly game, a five-dollar limit and, what, three raises maximum? The wins and losses pretty much average out over the course of a year, and nobody ever gets hurt too bad. Is that about right?"

"Yes."

"So you wouldn't expect to attract a mechanic, a card cheat, but he's not looking for the high rollers, he's looking for a game just like yours, where it's all good friends and nobody's got reason to get suspicious, and he can pick up two or three hundred dollars in a couple of hours without running any risks. I'm sure you're all decent poker players, but would you think to look for bottom dealing or a cold deck? Would you know if somebody was dealing seconds, even if you saw it in slow motion?"

"Probably not."

"Phil was probably doing a little cheating," I went on, "and that's probably what he did two weeks ago, and nobody spotted him. But he evidently crossed someone else somewhere along the line. Maybe he pulled the same tricks in a bigger game, or maybe he was just sleeping in the wrong bed, but someone knew he was coming here, turned up after the game was going, and rang the bell. He would have come in and called Phil out, but he didn't have to, because Phil answered the door."

"And the guy had a knife."

"Right," I said. "That's how it was, but it's another way an investigating officer might get confused. How did the guy know Phil was going to come to the door? Most times the host opens the door, and the rest of the time it's only one chance in five it'll be Phil. Would the guy be ready, knife in hand? And would Phil just open up without making sure who it was?"

I held up a hand. "I know, that's how it happened. But I think it might be worth your while to stage a more plausible scenario, something a lot easier for the cops to come to terms with. Suppose we forget the intruder. Suppose the story we tell is that Phil was cheating at cards and someone called him on it. Maybe some strong words were said and threats were exchanged. Phil went into his pocket and came out with a knife."

"That's . . ."

"You're going to say it's farfetched," I said, "but he'd probably have some sort of weapon on him, something to intimidate anyone who did catch him cheating. He pulls the knife and you react. Say you turn the table over on him. The whole thing goes crashing to the floor and he winds up sticking his own knife in his chest."

I walked across the room. "We'll have to move the table," I went on. "There's not really room for that sort of struggle where you've got it set up, but suppose it was right in the middle of the room, under the light fixture? Actually that would be a logical place for it." I bent down, picked up the throw rug, tossed it aside. "You'd move the rug if you had the table here." I bent down, poked at a stain. "Looks like somebody had a nosebleed, and fairly recently, or you'd have had the carpet cleaned by now. That can fit right in, come to think of it. Phil wouldn't have bled much from a stab wound to the heart, but there'd have been a little blood loss, and I didn't spot any blood at all where the body's lying now. If we put him in the right spot, they'll most likely assume it's his blood, and it might even turn out to be the same blood type. I mean, there are only so many blood types, right?"

I looked at them one by one. "I think it'll work," I said. "To sweeten it, we'll tell them you're friends of mine. I play in this game now and then, although I wasn't here when Phil was. And when the accident happened the first thing you thought of was to call me, and that's why there was a delay reporting the incident. You'd reported it to me, and I was on my way here, and you figured that was enough." I stopped for breath, took a moment to look each of them in the eye. "We'll want things arranged just right," I went on, "and it'll be a good idea to spread a little cash around. But I think this one'll go into the books as accidental death."

"They must have thought you were a genius," Elaine said.

"Or an idiot savant," I said. "Here I was, telling them to fake exactly what had in fact happened. At the beginning I think they may have thought I was blundering into an unwitting reconstruction of the incident, but by the end they probably figured out that I knew where I was going."

"But you never spelled it out."

"No, we maintained the fiction that some intruder stuck the knife in Ryman, and we were tampering with the evidence."

"When actually you were restoring it. What tipped you off?"

"The body blocking the door. The lividity pattern was wrong, but I was suspicious even before I confirmed that. It's just too cute, a body positioned where it'll keep a door from opening. And the table was in the wrong place, and the little rug had to be covering something, or why else would it be where it was? So I pictured the room the right way, and then everything sort of filled in. But it didn't take a genius. Any cop would have seen some wrong things, and he'd have asked a few hard questions, and the four of them would have caved in."

"And then what? Murder indictments?"

"Most likely, but they're respectable businessmen and the deceased was a scumbag, so they'd have been up on manslaughter charges and probably would have pleaded to a lesser charge. Still, a verdict of accidental death saves them a lot of aggravation."

"And that's what really happened?"

"I can't see any of those men packing a switch knife or pulling it at a card table. Nor does it seem likely they could have taken it away from Ryman and killed him with it. I think he went ass over teakettle with the table coming down on top of him and maybe one or two of the guys falling on top of the table. And he was still holding the knife, and he stuck it in his own chest."

"And the cops who responded——"

"Well, I called it in for them, so I more or less selected the responding officers. I picked guys you can work with."

"And worked with them."

"Everybody came out okay," I said. "I collected a few dollars from the four players, and I laid off some of it where it would do the most good."

"Just to smooth things out."

"That's right."

"But you didn't lay off all of it."

"No," I said, "not quite all of it. Give me your hand. Here."

"What's this?"

"A finder's fee."

"Three hundred dollars?"

"Ten percent," I said.

"Gee," she said. "I didn't expect anything."

"What do you do when somebody gives you money?"

"I say thank you," she said, "and I put it someplace safe. This is great. You get them to tell the truth, and everybody gets paid. Do you have to go back to Syosset right away? Because Chet Baker's at Mikell's tonight."

"We could go hear him," I said, "and then we

could come back here. I told Anita I'd probably have to stay over."

"Oh, goodie," she said. "Do you suppose he'll sing 'Let's Get Lost?' "

"I wouldn't be surprised," I said. "Not if you ask him nice."

I don't remember if he sang it or not, but I heard it again just the other day on the radio. He'd ended abruptly, that aging boy with the sweet voice and sweeter horn. He went out a hotel room window somewhere in Europe, and most people figured he'd had help. He'd crossed up a lot of people along the way and always got away with it, but then that's usually the way it works. You dodge all the bullets but the last one.

"Let's Get Lost." I heard the song, and not twenty-four hours later I picked up the *Times* and read an obit for a commodities trader named P. Gordon Fawcett, who'd succumbed to prostate cancer. The name rang a bell, but it took me hours to place it. He was the guy in the blazer, the man in whose apartment Phil Ryman stabbed himself.

Funny how things work out. It wasn't too long after that poker game that another incident precipitated my departure from the NYPD, and from my marriage. Elaine and I lost track of each other and caught up with each other some years down the line, by which time I'd found a way to live without drinking. So we get lost and found—and now we're married. Who'd have guessed?

My life's vastly different these days, but I can imagine being called in on just that sort of emergency—a man dead on the carpet, a knife in his chest, in the company of four poker players who only wish he'd disappear. As I said, my life's different, and I suppose I'm different myself. So I'd almost certainly handle it differently now, and what I'd probably do is call it in immediately and let the cops deal with it.

Still, I always liked the way that one worked out. I walked in on a cover-up, and what I did was cover up the cover-up. And in the process I wound up with the truth. Or an approximation of it, at least, and isn't that as much as you can expect to get? Isn't that enough?

For Sale
An April Woo Story

Leslie Glass

Leslie has written twelve novels, eight of which have featured NYPD Detective April Woo—except that she is now married and her name is Lt. April Woo Sanchez. The most recent Woo novel is *A Killing Gift* (Onyx, 2003). Prior to that Leslie departed from her series character to write a comic suspense novel called *Over His Dead Body* (Ballantine, 2003). This cautionary story features April and shows that even a seemingly benign game like dominoes can have dire consequences.

The For Sale sign sprouted over the weekend like an unwanted weed. It appeared on the right side of the low azalea hedge that lined both sides of the front walk to the neat Woo family two-story brick house in Astoria, Queens. Returning Sunday night from a wedding in New Jersey, old Sai Yuan Woo saw it first and went off like a New Year's rocket.

"Ayieee," she screamed. She was a small person, four feet eleven at most and thin as a reed. Her tightly permed hair was as black as onyx, her lips bright red, and her voice loud enough to stop a train. "Ayieee!"

It didn't stop this one, though. When the sign didn't disappear like a scared ghost, she tried staring it down. That didn't change it either. It still read FOR SALE. Sai scratched her head and tried to puzzle it out. If the sign had read HANDS OFF THE MERCHANDISE, or WET PAINT ON THE RAIL-

INGS, or DOUBLE YOUR MONEY BACK, she would have been at a loss to understand its meaning. She was not excellent at English and generally speaking did not aspire to useless knowledge. That was what children were for.

Sai Yuan Woo had only one child, a disappointment in some ways but brilliant and famous. Sergeant April Woo happened to be so smart that no crime in New York City could be solved without her. Even the mayor knew her name. Unfortunately that name was no longer Sergeant April Woo. Last spring she had married a Spanish ghost called Captain Mike Sanchez and also been promoted to lieutenant. So now she was Lieutenant April Woo Sanchez, and the name annoyed her mother almost as much her daughter's achievements made her proud.

Sai Yuan Woo was an old-style Chinese sixty, full of bound-feet-era superstitions and fears. In other words, she was a woman who believed in bad spirits and good ones and the power of the dragons that flew around in the skies, and she didn't like doing anything for herself. April still called her Skinny Dragon Mother because of her predilection for making mischief. Sai was the kind of foreign-born American citizen who never adapted. She had met her husband in Chinatown forty years ago, had worked in a dim sum restaurant that didn't have menus in Chinese, much less English. Her husband, Ja Fa Woo, read three of the four Chinese newspapers available in New York—not the one whose politics he abhorred—and like his wife, never became really fluent in English.

Still, for both of them, some words had penetrated deep, and *sale* was one. In fact, next to her best quality toy poodle, Dim Sum, which April had rescued from one of her murder cases, Sai considered Sale to be one of her very closest friends. It happened to be her clothing designer of choice, her favorite shoemaker. YARD SALE was her favorite store, better than the sidewalk vendors in Chinatown or Main Street of Flushing, Queens. Sai was nothing if not competitive, so discarded items from someone's home always presented an exciting opportunity to best an unwitting seller. To get a treasure for nothing—never mind whether or not she needed it—that was the best sale of all.

Sai's own single greatest treasure—her house—however, was definitely *not* for sale. "Ayieee," she screamed for the third time, pointing to the offense stuck in the dirt next to their front walk.

Ja Fa Woo lurched to a stop, squinted through his thick lenses, and attempted to penetrate the fog of a weekend's serious drinking in celebration of an old friend's son's wedding. The Chinese couple were on the final lap of their three-bus journey home from New Jersey. They were walking from the bus stop a few blocks from their home and both wheeled suitcases that were much larger than either of them had needed for the two-day stay. Traveling there, the suitcases had been stuffed with gifts. On the way home, they were a great deal lighter but still bulky and hard to manage.

Sai jabbed her husband with a sharp elbow. "Look, look," she screamed.

"What, what?" Ja Fa Woo peered down the street at his house. It was late October, so the red-for-luck azaleas were not in bloom. But the red berries of three healthy firethorn bushes had popped their golden husks to display the lucky color. Then he saw the sign and spat on the sidewalk. "Must be mistake," he said.

Ja Fa Woo was only two inches taller than his wife and, if possible, even thinner than she. He hurried home and abandoned his rolling suitcase by the front door. Then he returned for the sign. He grabbed it with both hands and tugged hard until it came out of the packed dirt.

He didn't even look at it. The real estate logo was a house with a Chinese name—Betty Chen—next to it, along with the number to call. It should have given the couple pause and made them curious enough to enquire, but the Chinese name didn't mean anything to them. they didn't know any Betty Chen; therefore she didn't exist for them.

Ja Fa Woo didn't talk much, so whenever he said something, Sai always agreed with him. He told her the sign was a big mistake, so that quiet Sunday afternoon she carried it down to the end of the block and threw it away in someone else's garbage can.

Two Sundays later, after she had forgotten all about it, the doorbell rang in the morning while she was watching a heart transplant on the surgery channel. She thought that it must be her new best friend, Mary Ling, almost fiancée of her tenant, Gao Wan, or her daughter who'd come early to take her shopping. Dim Sum ran to the door and barked up a storm.

"All right, all right, I'm coming," she yelled in Chinese and hurried to open the door. But April's new blue Jeep Cherokee was not parked out front there, and April was not at the door. Neither was Mary Ling. Instead, three little children were out there—ages maybe six to ten—and they charged the poodle, squealing with excitement.

"Is it ours? Is it ours?" they cried.

Sai jumped back as if prodded by some terrible electric police stun gun as a huge white ghost with yellow hair and a big grin on his face stuck his hand in her face.

"Hi, is this a bad time for a visit?" he asked.

"Yes. Bad time." Sai looked behind her to see if her husband was up. He worked late on Saturday nights and liked to sleep in on Sunday mornings. And all other mornings for that matter.

"I'm Howard Heller. My wife, Tootsie, Sarah, Josh and Tom. We're the new owners. Tom, be careful with that dog," he said to the smallest boy, who started pulling one of Dim's delicate back legs.

"Dad, can I have it? Can I have it?" the boy begged.

"No." Sai shook her head and grabbed the dog. "You have long number," she said and closed the door.

That rejection, however, didn't stop the man. He kept talking through the door. "Don't worry, we're not trying to sell you something. We're the new owners. We just came by to measure the rooms."

Sai had no idea what he was talking about, but she did know that sometimes people stole cute poodles. So she locked the three locks that April had installed after those two men pretending to be Con Edison workers came in and tried to kill them six months ago. She hid in the back of the house, in the kitchen. After a while, the white ghost gave up trying to talk to her and went away.

About three hours later April arrived. "Hi,

Ma, what's up?" she asked when Sai burst out of the door.

Of course, Sai couldn't tell her. Her heart swelled with love at the sight of the beautiful girl who'd broken all her dreams by marrying a Spanish. Who was now so important she had dinner with the police commissioner, and who had come up in the world so high that she didn't even live in Queens anymore. Sai gave that disappointing child her traditional greeting, a little punch on the arm, and started grumbling right away. "You're late. What kept you? Another murder?"

"No, not a murder today. Just traffic. What's new?" April couldn't even think of hugging her mother—who never ever hugged her—so she hugged the dog instead. Then she scooped up the pile of mail Skinny always left for her to analzye and deal with.

"Nothing new. Everything same," Sai said. "Is that a new dress?" And off they went to Flushing with no mention of the sign or the visitors.

A few days later the mailwoman rang the door and held out a letter with a green sticker on it.

"What's this?" Sai asked suspiciously.

"It's a registered letter." The postal worker happened to be Chinese and spoke to her in Cantonese.

"What if I don't want it?" Sai demanded, handing it back.

"Take it. Might be a check." The mailwoman held out her pen and pointed to the line where Sai had to sign.

Sai tilted her head to one side and studied the page on the clipboard that was half full of signatures. She thought the letter must be something important if she had to sign for it. But she wasn't sure she wanted it, so she decided to test the Chinese mailwoman to see how much she knew. Very carefully she wrote "no one home" in Chinese characters and handed the board back.

The woman looked at it, smiled and gave her the letter. That's how Sai knew it couldn't be so important, after all. Must be one of those appeals from the Democrats or the Republicans, or lawyers looking for business from accidents. She turned the letter over and saw the same little picture of a house as the one on the For Sale sign that had been in the front yard weeks ago. She was shocked and felt betrayed by the woman who came to her house every day bringing her mail. She threw the letter away without opening it. The house was not for sale.

But then she worried about it all morning. Maybe something was wrong. She might actually have suspected her sometimes-sneaky husband of wanting to move again since their worm daughter wasn't living with them any-more and wasn't ever coming back. But why move when they were not alone in the house? Her husband's underchef at the restaurant where he worked, Gao Wan, had moved into April's old apartment upstairs and was paying rent. Gao took out the garbage and changed the light bulbs whenever they burned out and did some shopping. And even his ABC (American-Born Chinese) girlfriend, Mary Ling, took the time to drink tea and play dominoes with her at least twice a week, which was more than her own daughter did. Sai decided it must be some ghost or devil working a mischief against her and began to guard her house. She stopped going out, even to take Dim Sum down to the end of the block for a walk.

When a second registered letter came several days later, Sai did not accept it at all, and that afternoon the telephone rang.

"Wei?" she answered warily.

"I am Betty Chen, Mrs. Woo. I am here. Please open the door," demanded a very bossy voice in Chinese.

Sai's heart fluttered with such annoyance that she did not even bother to pat her hair or put on her red lipstick. She was wearing brown plaid trousers, a look-like-silk blouse of purple and pink and green. Her multicolored knitted vest didn't match either her top or her bottom, but none of that bothered her. She marched to the door ready to fight. Outside was a big fat woman carrying a large black briefcase. She was wearing a gold pantsuit and wore a huge gold necklace, a gold watch, two gold bracelets and two diamond rings on each hand. Her face was broad, her eyes were heavily made up, and her powdered cheeks the color of flour. She almost looked like a white ghost instead of a Chinese one.

"What do you want?" Sai demanded in Chinese. She didn't like that woman one little bit.

"Grandmother, why didn't you answer my letters?" Betty Chen spoke good Chinese, but Sai knew without a doubt that this big fat woman covered in gold was an ABC, like April and Mary Ling, born in the USA and full of the kind of bossy confidence only truly felt by English speakers from birth. And although the voice of this ABC was tempered with pleasantness, Betty Chen's smile was as cold as the Arctic.

"Not for sale," Sai said angrily.

"I need to come in," Betty said sweetly.

"Not for sale," Sai repeated.

"We have to clear up this misunderstanding right now, grandmother. You can't ignore the situation any longer. We told you almost a month ago. The house is sold. The new owners are moving in next week. If you aren't out by Monday morning, you will be evicted."

"What's that?" Sai screamed.

"Evicted. Put out on the street. You don't want that, old woman, do you?" Betty Chen said all this in her bossy Chinese voice, and Sai's hammering heart almost burst with indignation.

"I don't know what you're talking about," she said angrily.

Betty Chen pushed past the little woman and paraded right into her house as if she owned it already. She opened her briefcase and handed Sai a bunch of papers. Sai could not read a single word on any of those papers, not even her name. *Sale* didn't appear either.

Then Betty Chen shook her finger at little Sai Yuan Woo. "The house is old. It isn't yours anymore. These papers prove it. Here's your signature, see? That should teach you not to be so reckless. Now, you have to go by Monday. It's the law."

"The law?" Sai trembled for the first time. What law?

"It says so right here. And don't try to tear this up. It won't make any difference. I have the originals."

"But where will I go?" Now Sai was really upset.

"Where you go is your business."

After Betty Chen left, Sai returned to the kitchen where the surgery channel was showing a breast augmentation. Sai had seen it many times before, but she watched the empty bag inserted into the flap in the double-stupid patient's breast. Sai's heart hammered and her breath caught as she watched the breast swell when the bag was pumped up with water. By the time the breast was as plump as a duck and all sewn up, she knew what she had to do.

"Lieutenant Woo Sanchez." April answered her cell phone on the third ring.

"*Ni*, when is baby coming?" Sai shrieked at her in Chinese.

"Ma?" April took the phone away from her ear. It was early Tuesday afternoon. She was in the Emergency Room of St. Luke's Hospital, too distracted for a conversation with her Skinny Dragon Mother. She had just informed George and Freda Allen, the unfortunate parents of Tommy Allen, a college freshman, that their beloved son had died that morning in the fraternity house that was rushing him. It was a bad moment. The worst. The parents were hysterical, unable to process the news that their only son had lapsed into a coma after a weekend of binge drinking.

"But hazing isn't allowed," the father kept saying. "He was fine on Friday."

Further, they couldn't believe that Tommy's buddies had left him on the floor in a back room, lying in his vomit while they watched *Monday*

Night Football, then went to bed, thinking he'd just sleep it off.

"That's murder. It's as good as murder," George Allen said numbly. "Are you sure it's him?"

April was trying to explain that it was when her mother cut in again.

"*Ni*," Skinny screamed at her. "Listen, we're moving in to take care of baby."

"What baby?" Puzzled, April turned away from the weeping couple.

"Your baby. The house is sold. We're moving in with you this weekend," Sai informed her. Loud, very loud.

April blinked. She didn't have a baby. She'd just gotten married. And her parents couldn't move to her and Mike's house in Westchester. No one spoke Chinese there, it was too far to walk to the store, and there was no easy way for her father to get to his job in the city. Besides, she and Mike had just moved in a few months ago and hadn't even finished furnishing it. It was impossible. What was her mother thinking?

"Did you hear me, *ni*? House is sold."

"You sold the house? Are you nuts?" April had two thoughts almost at the same time. The first was: If the house was sold, she wouldn't be responsible for the mortgage anymore. Yippee. Her second thought was having her parents come to live with them was out of the question. Impossible. Forget it!

Mrs. Allen's knees buckled, and April turned back to her first priority, her job. "Ma, I have to call you back," she said.

"Don't call back. Just come home," Sai answered with a little sob in her voice.

April was afraid her mother had finally gone over the edge. She found a hospital social worker to deal with the grief-stricken Allens and went outside to meet her driver. Detective Woody Baum was on the phone collecting names of students and university officials who would be involved in the case. Then they drove over to the university to start investigating the circumstances surrounding Tommy Allen's death. They spent the rest of the afternoon interviewing frightened college students who didn't all tell the same story. But a few details did emerge. The boys had been drinking hard, and the older ones had stored the pass-outs and pukers in empty bedrooms. One freshman claimed that he'd known Tommy was in trouble early on and had begged for 911 intervention, but the older brothers didn't want any trouble and refused. Many angles would have to be looked at before the case would be resolved. Meanwhile, the frat house was closed, and an autopsy was being performed on Tommy to see if any other illegal substances might have contributed to his death.

At nine p.m., Woody drove April back to the precinct where she was CO of the detective unit. She filled in the second whip who was on duty, Connie Morton, distributed some new complaints that had come in since her absence, then said good night. Out on the street, she collected her Jeep from its spot out front, drove across town and then across the Fifty-ninth Street Bridge to find out what bug had bitten her mother.

At that time of the evening the traffic wasn't too bad on the bridge or in the quiet Astoria neighborhood, so she made it home in less than twenty minutes. She found Skinny Dragon in the kitchen, cooking dinner and watching trauma surgery with the sound off. April stopped in the doorway to inhale one of the most delicious aromas in the whole world. A roasting duck. Right away she knew that whatever the trouble was, it was big.

"Ma, what's going on?" she asked suspiciously.

Skinny Dragon Mother was dressed in rice paddy peasant pants and jacket and didn't answer. She banged down a dinner plate on the kitchen table and threw some chopsticks beside it. The linoleum-topped table was a new one; the matching chairs were new, too. So were the fixtures in the downstairs bathroom and the paint job in the living room. The fight in the house last spring had made a big bloody mess, but the three-bedroom house had been spruced up a good deal since then, courtesy of the guilty Mike Sanchez. Two perpetrators in a murder case had followed his fiancée home to her parents' house and tried to kill them all.

Now the prosperous looking house belied the peasant appearance of its owner. In dangerous times, Skinny Dragon always dressed like a coolie to fool the gods into thinking she was too poor to be of interest. April inhaled the enticing smells of home and exhaled the sorrow of the Allens and all other real world miseries. She took off her leather jacket and hung her shoulder bag with her entire life in it—her gold shield, ID, notebooks, cell phone, address book, tissues and lipsticks, rubber gloves, plastic evidence bags, and extra gun—over the back of the chair. Then she sat in one of the new chairs and waited for enlightenment or food, whichever came first.

An hour later, stuffed with delicate flavor crab wontons, Singapore noodles, hacked duck with hoisin sauce on fried lettuce and a number of other favorite foods, April put down her chopsticks for the last time.

"What's this about the house?" she asked at last.

Sai pressed her thin lips together and shook her head. "Betty Chen bad person," she said.

"Who's Betty Chen?"

"She sold house."

April pushed her chair back into the kitchen's work space. "She couldn't sell the house, Ma. It isn't hers to sell."

"Sold it for Mary," Sai explained.

"Mary Ling?" April flashed to the girl whom Gao Wan was trying to marry, probably for citizenship, not for love. Mary was thirty-five, three years older than April, a reasonably attractive girl who'd slacked off at school, then failed in real estate and travel offices and a bunch of other professions. But that never seemed to bother her, and she always had money for expensive clothes and jewelry. At the sound of Mary's name, April was suddenly deeply suspicious.

"What's she got to do with it?" she demanded.

Sai's face colored. "She say won the house in bet."

April's mouth dropped open. She couldn't believe what she was hearing. "Dad gambled the house to Mary Ling?"

"Shh, don't tell."

Sai brushed a pile of imaginary crumbs off the table.

The way she did it and the way her eyes

avoided April's, plus the quality of the meal she'd just served, told April that it was not her father who'd been the big fool, but her mother. "What happened?" she asked quietly.

Skinny Dragon gave her a guilty look, then handed over the papers that Betty Chen had left at the house that morning. April took a long time looking them over. Finally she shook her head and sighed. It was worse than anything she could imagine.

"Do you know what these papers say?" she asked.

"House sold?" Skinny asked almost meekly.

"Ma, did you have any idea your house is worth over three hundred thousand dollars?" April tapped on the table with an angry finger.

"Ayieee," Skinny screamed. "Three hundred!"

"Three hundred thirty-five thousand is the purchase price," she said sternly, appalled that this could happen after Mike had worked so hard to get the place cleaned up for them. All the years of ownership and her paying the mortgage, all their efforts and money were gone in a few moments of foolishness. She felt like the parent of very stupid children.

"Three hundred and thirty-five thousand. What were you thinking?" she demanded. Then, "What would you have gotten if you won?"

The Dragon finally stopped pretending to

clean the table and sat down. "Don't tell your father," she begged. *This was a terrible loss of face.* Her expression said it all.

"Ma, you signed away the house. How can you hide this from him?"

"We come to your house. We take care of you, Mike, your baby." She had it all planned out.

You can't live with us. April thought that, but didn't say it out loud. A lot of things couldn't be said out loud. Her mother was an idiot, a compulsive gambler who was easily taken in—a triple-stupid menace! She didn't say any of that.

"Ma, you have to stop this. People don't just give their houses away" was what she did say.

Too late. The Dragon's eyes flashed. "Oh, yes they do give away. What about your house?"

"That was different," April said quietly.

"Gave you house for nothing. What's the difference?" Skinny argued.

"Well, it wasn't completely for nothing. And there's a big difference." April's full stomach churned. It desperately wanted to return the hacked duck, heave it right back at her impossible mother who did everything she could to make life difficult. April tried swallowing her anger, but it didn't go down.

"I didn't win the house gambling," she said. "I solved a mystery—I recovered a lot of money for the owner."

"Same thing," Skinny snorted.

"No, Ma, it isn't the same thing. Kathy didn't live in her house. You live in your house. You didn't intend to sell it. Kathy had a big gain; you have only loss. Big loss. I have a loss, too, now."

In fact, April held the mortgage on the house, had paid the taxes, and expected to own it some day herself. She should have made the profit. She shrugged that part off. She couldn't really lose what she'd never owned. Skinny Dragon sniffed and looked down at her hands. The knuckles were swollen with arthritis, and April could tell they hurt. Suddenly she softened with ten thousand years of filial duty and collective Chinese guilt. She knew her mother was lonely, wanted companionship. Maybe it was her fault that she'd not spent enough time with her. "You didn't mean to gamble away your house, did you, Ma?" she asked softly.

The once powerful Dragon, who was now only a foolish old woman, shook her head. No, she hadn't meant to gamble away her house. She gazed at her daughter with deep shame. "You good girl, *ni*. We move in with you Saturday, *hao*?" *Okay?* she asked.

April was not going to say *hao*, because it wasn't okay at all. She patted her mother's arthritic hand. "We'll see" was as far as she'd go on the subject.

* * *

"Ay, *querida*, what's going on?" Mike Sanchez stopped short just inside the kitchen door. It was one thirty a.m. He'd just gotten home from his job in the city. He'd put his new car in his new garage and found his stunning new wife wide awake, smelling like a bower of roses and wearing the lacy red teddy and negligee he'd bought her last Valentine's Day. This was the kind of thing he fantasized about daily but didn't often get. April was a busy woman, up before dawn and usually exhausted by midnight. Something had to be up.

Mike was the commanding officer of the Seventeenth Precinct in Manhattan, which covered the East Side from Fifth Avenue to the East River—the United Nations area in the Thirties up to the Fifty-ninth Street Bridge. The former head of the NYPD's Homicide Task Force, he'd worn a leather jacket and cowboy boots for fifteen years. Now he was back in uniform, getting his administration training and taking a little vacation from murder. His hours were better than April's, but tonight the handsome precinct captain with the black hair and dashing mustache looked tired.

"How about an intimate massage?" April asked demurely.

Mike raised an eyebrow. Something was definitely up. "Is this a feminine ploy?"

"Maybe." She smiled and reached for his gun

to disarm him, and he laughed as her hand traveled below the belt.

"What's the occasion?" he murmured.

"How about just glad to see you?" He laughed again, not entirely buying it.

Nonetheless, he was more than willing to switch gears from top cop to Latin lover in five seconds flat. April shivered with delight at a deep kiss he gave her and led him to the sofa in the living room where there was a cosy fire in the fireplace. For a while they forgot pretty much everything but each other.

Then after a long hiatus, Mike stretched and inquired about food. "That was very nice, *mi amor*. Thank you. Is there any food?"

"Thank you, too. Of course there's food." April struggled into her red teddy, covered it with his shirt, then padded in bare feet into the kitchen. In a moment or two, he followed her. It was only after she had set the table with her mother's excellent dinner leftovers that she dropped the bomb.

"Looks like my mom gambled her house away in a mahjong game. The new owner sold it out from under them, and they're getting evicted Monday." She said all this as casually as she could.

"What?" Mike nearly dropped a plate full of dumplings.

"They want to move in with us over the weekend," she added slowly.

"Just a little minute, *querida*. I need more information than that. What happened?" Mike shivered as he waited for an answer.

April took a second to peer out the window. It was black out there now, but in the daytime there was a nice view of the patio, the lawn furniture, the built-in barbecue. Inside the homey kitchen it was toasty warm. She shook her head at how much meaning there was in a house, each one the foundation of some family's security. The house was the most powerful of all symbols of safety. Deeply ashamed of her ignorant mother's foolishness, she answered the question.

"Looks like Mary Ling got Mom's signature on a transfer of property. Mary put the house on the market, and it sold a couple of weeks ago. Mom's very embarrassed about it. She just told me today. The closing's Monday." That about covered it.

"Oh, God!" Disgusted, April's handsome naked husband hurried out of the kitchen and disappeared up the stairs, without even a glance at the enticing food he'd left behind.

"Damn." April sat down at the kitchen table and waited. About ten minutes later he returned with wet hair, dressed in jeans and a sweatshirt, back to cop again.

"Sorry," April murmured. She was more than sorry.

He waved away the apology. "Just run this by me again. Mary is Gao's girlfriend. Gao is your dad's protégé in the restaurant, right?"

She nodded.

"Was this something they conspired together?"

"I don't know," April confessed. It hadn't occurred to her that a just-off-the-boat like Gao could even think of plotting to take her father's job and his house all in his first year in America. That would be some trick. She didn't like this at all.

"Better find out and get it sorted out," Mike told her, finally glancing at the food with some interest.

Then he shook his head. He wasn't going to get vocal about her mother's invasion plan, but April gathered it was a "no" on the Dragon's moving in. "Do whatever you have to do." He gave her a sneaky little smile. It just so happened that he knew her too well.

After he had made love and eaten well and put his foot down about his wife's mother, Mike slept like a baby. With two new investigations pending, however, April didn't sleep at all. She was worried about the Tommy Allen case. And ten thousand questions about her mother's devastating indiscretion bombarded her steadily throughout the night. In her mother's situation, it started with some legal basics, like where was the deed on the house and how could a deal close without her father's signature? Surely he didn't want to sign away his half interest. She wondered how they planned to pull it off without his signature. As far as April knew, Skinny hadn't even told her husband. None of it made sense.

Further, Skinny hadn't told her the exact sum of her debt to Mary Ling. April thought maybe she could attack the problem that way. But what if the house itself had been the bet? That was puzzling. April just couldn't imagine her mother betting her house. Skinny was a dime bettor, a quarter bettor, not a house bettor. And why would her mother wait until the house was already sold, almost until the moment of eviction, to confess? Didn't she trust her own daughter to fix it? Mike was right; she needed to get the whole story.

Wednesday morning she'd planned a totally different kind of day off. But instead of sleeping in, then taking care of her own business, she paid an early visit to Betty Chen in Long Island City, where the real estate office was in a storefront on a busy street. As soon as she parked the Jeep and crossed the sidewalk, she saw a photo of her parents' house among many others in the window. The house with the wisteria trained in an arch around the front door and the decorative fans over the windows had a sold sticker on it. In the photo, the wisteria was in bloom, and it was now November. April wondered where the picture had come from and who had taken it.

Inside, a well-dressed middle-aged Chinese woman was busy on the phone. The plaque on her desk read BETTY CHEN. April stood in front of the desk. As Betty Chen listened to the speaker on the other end, she shrewdly evaluated her customer. The diamond engagement ring, the wedding band, the chic suit and good haircut persuaded the real estate agent to end her call quickly.

"I'm Betty. Do sit down and tell me what you're looking for," she said unctuously.

"I'm April Woo. You have my parents' house for sale." April decided to open with the little guns and hold back the nuclear attack for now.

"Oh, Miss Woo." Betty Chen smiled a big fake smile. "So glad you stoped by. Maybe you're looking for a new place for your parents? I would be glad to help you find something suitable. Something smaller, maybe?" She did not display the slightest discomfort at the situation.

April did not return the smile. "I hold the mortgage on the house—" she began.

Betty cut her off. "Yes, yes, of course, and the

mortgage will be paid in full at the closing. I can assure you, you will have no liability in the matter after the deal is concluded." She closed her lips into a tight smile.

"Well, that's not the issue. You should have informed me of the listing," April told her.

Betty pushed some papers around her desk, too busy to comment.

"My father, who is half owner of the house, has no idea the house was for sale. My mother didn't know until your visit yesterday. I just found out this morning. I'm concerned there may be an attempted fraud in the sale."

"Well, that's not possible." Betty Chen came to life with the threat of trouble. "Mary Ling has proof that everything was settled very amicably between your mother and her. These things happen. Your mother knew perfectly well what she was doing. Mary has ownership of the house. We've had no problems whatsoever . . ."

"My mother had no idea what you were up to. That's why you had no trouble," April said flatly.

"That's ridiculous. The For Sale sign went up in plain view; the house was shown. Five couples saw it. It's a lovely house, Miss Woo. It sold the first day." Up went those shoulders.

April stared. "A For Sale sign went up?"

"Of course," Betty said imperiously. "We did everything properly. We informed your parents the house had been sold by registered letter. The new owners came to visit her several weeks ago. Sellers' remorse is not uncommon, especially with old people. My condolences at your difficulties," she said sweetly.

April had a lot of experience keeping her emotions under control. This affront was not the worst she had endured in her years as a cop. But she needed to know a lot more about those "difficulties" to which Betty Chen referred. "Did my mother produce a deed for the house?" she asked.

"Ah, no. Apparently, it's been lost. We have requested a copy. We'll have one by the end of the week."

"My father is the co-owner. Do you have his signature on the transfer?" April was going to nail her.

Betty Chen blinked. "I understand your family's circumstances; I spoke to your mother. It is unfortunate, but what can I do?" she asked as if she were powerless.

"You can't close the deal without both signatures. Naturally the legal aspects of your listing and your agreement with Miss Ling will have to be reviewed."

"Legal aspects? We do everything properly here." Betty bristled.

"A title search, I believe, will show that no

legal transfer of property has been made," April
snapped.

"Ah, this is something you will have to talk to
Mary about. I'm sure she can fill you in on the
circumstances." Betty Chen's phone rang and
she picked it up, giving April one last fake smile
as she left.

April's anger escalated as she crossed the
sidewalk and found her car. Registered letters?
A For Sale sign? Skinny Dragon had neglected to
mention them. She was in a rage, but she was
also worried now. Her mother had held a few
things back.

You'd think it wouldn't be so easy to find a
scammer like Mary Ling in the haystack of a
borough like Queens with all its millions of people, but April Woo wasn't a detective for nothing. Only an hour later she found Mary getting
a manicure in the beauty parlor where she'd
once answered the phone. Her toenails were already finished. Rolled-up paper towels were
threaded between her toes, the nails a color that
April could only call black. When Mary saw
April, her fat pillow lips pursed into an *O* as she
glanced quickly away.

"What would you like?" asked the young
woman at the desk.

April shook her head at the menu of services
offered there and took the chair at the manicure

station next to Mary's, forcing Mary to speak first. Mary was a tall thin girl with long, dyed-brown hair, a too high forehead and shifty eyes.

"April, what a surprise. How's married life treating you?" she asked in a lazy voice.

"What's going on?" April asked coldly.

"I'm having my nails done." Mary exchanged amused looks with her manicurist.

"I mean about my parents' house. This is not a joke. My family has been very good to you. What do you think you're doing to them?"

Mary gave her a shocked look. "I wouldn't hurt your parents for anything in the world. Your mother loves me like a daughter. She wants me and Gao to be as lucky and happy in our lives as you are. It's too bad if you're jealous." She tossed her head.

April was stunned by this impudence but didn't want to betray any weakness by letting her know she'd hit a nerve. "Then why don't you tell me what happened," she said softly.

"You know very well what happened," Mary snapped back. "You're always busy. Never have time for anybody. I was there every day, taking care of her—"

"Gambling," April cut in.

"Not gambling. We played dominoes. You know how she loves that."

Uh-oh. April kept her eyes neutral. "Yes, she

does. But you still haven't told me what happened."

Mary watched her manicurist apply the base coat to very long fingernails. "It was her idea to bet so much, not mine. A thousand a game. I guess it was her way to give me something. I love the woman as much as my own mom."

That couldn't be very much, April thought, since Mary's own mother wouldn't let her into the house. "You bet in thousands?" she said calmly, knowing this couldn't be true.

"Well, it was fun. And when I asked her to pay up, she offered the house." Mary shrugged. "What can you do? You know how stubborn she is." She blew on the first coat of black.

This certainly couldn't be true. April frowned. "I'm trying to figure this out. You and my mother were betting in thousands?"

"Mm-hmm. That's right."

"And how much did she owe you when you called her on it?"

"Two hundred thousand." Mary blew some more on those black nails.

"But Mary, you know my mother doesn't have two hundred thousand dollars."

"Well, she signed an IOU."

April nodded, although she knew her mother well enough to be sure Skinny Dragon could never have done this willingly. April had seen many incidents of people duped by scammers—

from penny-ante stuff on the street to gypsies descending like locusts on whole neighborhoods, to Wall Street fraud of vast proportions. Greed ruled everywhere. She took a breath to calm herself. "I'd like to see this IOU."

"No problem." Mary studied her nails.

"Now!" April said sharply.

"Don't worry. I have it," she said airily.

"Mary, if you don't show me the IOU, the sale isn't going to happen." April wasn't on duty, but she wore her gun strapped to her waist. In a subtle movement, she shifted her position, and the gun peeped out of her jacket.

Mary clicked her tongue at the sight of it. "I have the document, April. I'm sure you've seen it yourself. This is all on the up-and-up, so don't even think about trying to threaten me. It's not my problem if your mommy loves me more than you. It's yours."

"Mary, listen to me. If I don't get that IOU within the hour, I'm going to take you and your friend Betty Chen down for fraud."

"Oh, please." Mary rolled her eyes. "Don't play the cop. This is real life."

"You know, one more thing. The house is seling for three thirty-five. I gather you had planned to pay my parents what they would be owed on the remaining amount."

Mary gave her a blank stare. "After the mortgage and broker's fee and the taxes I doubt there will be very much."

April saw it differently. She figured that not-so-much might have come to as much as fifty thousand. She shook her head. Mary didn't seem concerned.

"April, I know this must be hard for you to swallow, but you don't have to lose face with this. I won't embarrass you," she said. She just didn't get it.

"We'll see."

An hour later April drove home to her mother's almost-sold house where Skinny was surprised to see her.

"Are we moving, *ni*?" she asked.

April didn't see any boxes around the living room or dining room. "Where's Dad?"

Skinny cocked her head to the bedroom. "Not up yet. You mad, *ni*?" For once she seemed concerned about it.

"Why didn't you tell me about the For Sale sign, the registered letters, your betting a thousand dollars a game?" April demanded as gently as she could. Just testing everyone's story.

"I didn't bet a thousand dollars. Aieyee. You crazy?" Skinny started screaming in Chinese. "You think I'm crazy?"

The thought had crossed April's mind. "Shh,

Ma. I'm not deaf." Actually, she was kind of re-lieved. She did know her own mother, after all.

But Skinny couldn't stop shrieking. "I didn't bet thousand dollars."

"How about two *hundred thousand* dollars?"

"What? What?" Skinny started hopping up and down. The dog was barking. "Two hundred thousand? You crazy?" Even in Chinese she didn't have much of a vocabulary.

"Sit down, Ma. Why didn't you tell me weeks ago?" Back in control, April was feeling better and better.

"I don't know what happened."

"Mary thinks you gave her the house."

"What? What?" Skinny was off again. Rant-ing and raving.

"Okay, okay. I believe you. But you were bet-ting with her. You signed a paper. What did you think the paper was?"

"IOU," Skinny said.

"What for?"

"Two hundred dolla." This she said in En-glish.

"Two hundred dollars?" April repeated in Chinese.

Skinny nodded and looked ashamed. She knew it was a lot to lose. "We never settle up, just play. It was a game."

Turned out to be a very big game. "What about the other paper?" April asked.

Dim Sum whined and Skinny picked her up, shaking her head. She didn't know what April was talking about.

"Didn't you sign another paper?"

Skinny shrugged. "Maybe, a petition. Long time ago."

"Mary gave you a petition, what for?"

"Maybe. Are we coming to live with you and the baby, *ni*?"

"Oh, you're happier in your own house, Ma," April said. Oddly she was relieved to find out that her mother didn't really love Mary Ling more than her. Mary obviously knew how to push all the right buttons. She wasn't going to ask her mother again what petition.

"You good girl, *ni*. You fix?" Skinny said, giving her what passed for a hug.

April nodded at the clumsy mangling. "You bet. I fix."

As soon as she had her mother calmed down, she marched upstairs to her old apartment and banged on the door. Gao Wan opened quickly. "Hey, April." His face lit up at the sight of her. He was a good-looking guy. She could see why Mary was after him.

"You getting married, Gao, and moving out?" April asked.

"Huh?" Gao seemed surprised.

"It's not a trick question. You must know the house has been sold. You have to get out."

"I was sorry to hear it. I like it here." He seemed to mean it.

"Too bad you have to go back to China then, Gao."

"No, I'm staying here." He looked confused.

"No, you're not. I'm reporting you to the INS. They'll arrest you and put you in a detention camp. After about six months, they'll deport you. People who commit crimes can't stay here in the US. You knew that, didn't you?"

"What? I didn't commit a crime. What crime?" He shuddered. Clearly he didn't want to go back to China.

"You tried to make nearly a quarter of a million dollars by stealing my parents' house. You bastard, you're lucky I don't shoot your balls off, too."

Gao recoiled at her words. "Steal this house? Are you crazy?"

Why was everyone calling her crazy? April shook her head. "Mary gambled with my mother. She didn't tell you she cheated?"

Gao's eyes opened wide. "I don't know about it."

"I'm going to send her to prison." April's face was cold as stone. "And don't think about packing your things and running away. I can catch you wherever you go."

Feeling better and better, she turned around

to go back downstairs. She was going to nail all the rats.

"Please. Wait a minute," Gao called after her and touched her on the shoulder before she could get away. She turned to look at him.

"I didn't do it. How can I prove I wouldn't do such a thing?" Gao had tears in his eyes, and she wanted to believe him. She really did. He was her dad's protégé, after all. Maybe her mother would trust a snake, but she liked to think her father wouldn't. What if Gao was telling the truth? Mary was a pretty good liar about Skinny Dragon. She pretended to leave, then hestitated.

"Well, maybe I can help you if you get the evidence for me," she said slowly.

"What evidence?" Gao began to look hopeful. "I don't know about evidence."

"Mary got an IOU from my mother. The thing is she changed the numbers of the debt from two hundred to two hundred thousand. That's fraud. On the basis of it, she tried to get the house. You can go to prison for that."

April was already putting together the case in her mind. She would look into Betty Chen's business pretty carefully. Since Betty had tried a phony property transfer once, she might have tried it before. But even if this was a first offense for her, clearly she and Mary had conspired to defraud the Woos out of their house to sell it.

Too bad that the old couple's lack of understanding of the langauge and the law was counterbalanced by their daughter's familiarity with it. This made her feel good.

Gao was nodding solemnly. "Okay, April, I can get it. Then I won't talk to her again." He shuddered a second time, either thinking of prison, or China, or what might have happened to her parents. Or maybe he was thinking of a marriage he'd escaped. "I'll make it up to them. I'll make it up to you, too. I promise you'll be proud of me."

"We'll see," April sniffed. She wasn't letting anyone off easy.

When she was finished scaring Gao to death, April skipped downstairs to see her mother again. Skinny was back in front of the surgery channel, watching a skin graft on a burn patient. "You fix?" she asked again. "You leaving?" She looked at her daughter searchingly, not daring even to offer food.

"No, Ma. I have some time." It was her day off, after all. April sank down on one of the comfortable new kitchen chairs. "I'm tired. I need to relax. How about some tea, some food and a game of dominoes?" She hadn't played since she was about seven; she didn't think it was going to be a problem to lose.

A former restaurant employee, Skinny

Dragon Mother hurried to fill the order of the child she used to call worm daughter. April sighed, snagged the remote and turned off the TV.

Snake Eyes

Jonathon King

Florida journalist King made a splash with his
first novel, *The Blue Edge of Midnight* (Dutton,
2002), nominated for an Edgar Award. Continuing the ripple effect in the mystery genre pond
is his *A Visible Darkness* (Dutton, 2003). For this
story, however, he abandons his series character, Max Freeman, and take us back in time to
the '20s, an era when casinos were part of every
landscape, even snake- and alligator-infested
Florida—where reptiles came in all shapes and
sizes.

He saw them coming. Over the high grass a swirl of dust spun up on the horizon, rising on the midday heat. He squinted into hard sunlight and timed the movement. *Car*, he thought. *Maybe two.* Behind him, to the west, towering clouds with anvil-flat bottoms moved across the sky from the Everglades toward the ocean, soaking up moisture and turning bruised and dark as they came. In his hand was the twisted neck of a burlap sack and he could feel the writhing of thick animal muscle inside of it.

He pulled the wide-brimmed hat from his head and wiped the sweat from his eyes and then looked down, refocusing on the shadows of a saw palmetto clumped up beside him. The snakes were not forgiving of a man's inattention. And contrary to legend, diamondbacks did not always sound their dry rattle before they struck. He stood watching both the trailing dust of approaching men and the half-hidden maw of a gopher hole, where the rattlers in this open ridge country liked to nest. He'd been in this part of south Florida long enough to know either one could bring trouble. And as in all gambles, anticipation and assessment are always key.

Four days earlier, on a dirt street in Miami, he had arrived on a corner at the edge of town with a handbill: "Wanted: Men Not Afraid of Snakes and Reptiles. Cash Money!" He'd joined two dozen others at the printed address. Most of the men who showed up were in their twenties and thirties, anxious and fidgety, their feet shuffling and hands busy around cigarettes and small packages of chew. Some wore their tweed suits, the color faded from the sun, the collars and cuffs rubbed soft at the edges. Others were in suspenders and caps but still scuffed about in stitched, hard-leather shoes. Street shoes. City shoes.

O'Hanlon had been in Miami less than a week, fresh off the train from his Brooklyn neighborhood, and he could already spot the "binder boys." They were the young, slick-talking hustlers from the city who'd come to the land boom of Florida. They'd heard on cold northern sidewalks that there were fortunes to be made in the sun. Packing their cardboard suitcases and carrying a roll of savings or a stake gathered from family and friends, they'd come south. In a place gone real-estate mad they'd buy a chunk of unseen land and then sell it for profit days later, long before they ever had to make a payment. The "binder" on the property would change hands ten times until the last fool left holding it was stuck with the inflated bill, unable to find another buyer.

It was high-stakes gambling, not high finance. O'Hanlon had learned the scam from the shoeshine boy outside his flophouse hotel. He also learned that by this late fall of 1925, the boom was going bust. It had been a cleanout for the ones who had arrived early and who had money to begin with. No doubt some nameless butter-and-egg man from Yonkers fell into luck and came out sharp. But by this time the binder boys had fallen to O'Hanlon's level, scrounging after any odd job they could just to buy a meal.

At the morning gathering he watched the group, scrutinizing each man's hands, reading their eyes when they turned to speak to one another and especially when the conversation went quiet.

"You can always measure a man by his hands and eyes," O'Hanlon's father had taught him. "Don't even need to see 'em get inta the ring. If they're scared, it's in their eyes, son. If they're weak, it's in their hands."

He had heard it hundreds of times in his father's boxing gym on Delacourt. He had grown up in that gym, watching men bring their dreams in off the street, watching the ones whose ambition or determination or desperation drove them. He'd also seen the ones who let that same motivation leak away and watched others have it beaten out of them. The many who were without talent or were just plain lazy left without scars, their pride put in its proper place before the real fighting started. The few with skill labored and learned and could raise a dozen expectations with their potential. But he had only witnessed one champion, then seen him fall under the thumb of promoters and handlers and gamblers. The rich got richer, the rest of us worked and watched.

His father's lessons were still with him that morning when a battered Model T truck pulled to the corner. A gray-bearded man with red suspenders climbed out of the cab and then swung himself up into the truck bed. With a voice scratched with age and handrolled tobacco, he introduced himself as Rattlesnake Pete. O'Hanlon took in the old man's hands, the fingers knurled and twisted, two of them missing half their length. He could see that despite their damage, they were not weak hands.

"Any you all boys ever catched you a snake?" he said, his drawl coming straight out of Alabama. The group of men had started to gather but no one offered an answer. The man called Pete did not bother to look up for any nods of assent or bragging. His attention was on the truck-bed floor where he'd bent to hoist a burlap bag.

"Ya'll work with me an' we got ten acres of brush land to clear outta rattlers," he went on while untwisting the neck of the bag. A half dozen of the men narrowed their eyes on the movement of Mr. Pete's hands and another half dozen, most of the binder boys, took a subtle step back.

"I pay you fifty cent a snake and that'll beat pickin' beans any day, boys," he said, still looking into the hole of the bag opening and then suddenly stabbing his hand in.

"Course, this ain't no bean neither," he said as his fist came out with a slick, writhing ribbon of flesh.

Six more men stepped two full steps back. A few stayed rooted. They were not necessarily brave men. The promise of fifty cents a snake was the glue. Mr. Pete now focused his attention back on the group, looking each of them in the eyes, going face to face. Then, without a word of embellishment or warning, he flung the snake down into the dirt, and two more of the men jumped back while the beast coiled itself in the shadow of the truck bumper and began to vibrate.

"All right, boys," the snakeman said, climbing down from the bed and moving more smoothly and surely than a man his age should have. "Ain't no danger if ya'll do what I learn ya."

O'Hanlon and three others who'd stayed close cut their eyes to old Pete's movements, O'Hanlon studying the footwork, watching the body parts closest to snake. The old man eased in, bending at the knee and never letting his eyes leave the rattler's head.

"Oncet ya'll know where he's at, just keep his attention. They's just stupid animals, boys. Ain't got nothin' in they heads but meanness and belly hunger and they already know ya'll too big to eat."

Now on his knee only a yard from the snake, the old man raised one hand and the reptile's unblinking eyes locked onto the movement and rotated its head to match its slow path. O'Hanlon could hear the heavy breathing of the man next to him and the scuffle of feet farther back of the onlookers now trying to gain a view. With the animal's head now focused on his left hand, the old snake man drifted his right hand more slowly to circle back behind the floating head.

"Ain't a magician nor card player don't know how to git you lookin' at the one thing whilst they trickin' you with the other," old Pete said, staring intently at the snake's head and sliding his left hand to further distract it. If the beast did not follow his left, the snake man kept his right hand still and waited for the snake's attention to return to the movement before closing the gap. The breath sound next to O'Hanlon had stopped. Or maybe it was his own.

"Ya'll old enough to know THAT!" old Pete suddenly yelped, simultaneously flicking his right hand across ten inches of space and snatching up the snake just behind its spade-shaped head. "Ain't ya'll?"

The man called Pete stood up and extended his arm. From his fist the rattler hung, curling its body frantically into a series of desperate S-shapes, its unhinged mouth glistening wide and white and angry.

The man beside O'Hanlon was shaking his head in appreciation and the group behind began to mumble.

"Fifty cent for five minutes of work, boys," Pete said, now with a teasing light in his eye. "Anybody that's game, climb on up into the truck."

Three of them made it into the field. Rattlesnake Pete was not nearly as dramatic when showing the newcomers how to flush a gopher hole with kerosene to bring the snakes writhing and blind out into the sunlight. He'd armed them with long-handled, close-tined pitchforks if they wanted. The old man had been hired, he said, to clear the scrub just north and west of Miami of all its rattlers. The buyer of the land was to begin construction on what he promised would be the finest horse-racing track and paddock south of Lexington, and just the thought of snakes and thoroughbred horses together would not do.

With an early morning sun already burning deep into his shoulders and the exposed angles of his nose and cheeks and forehead, O'Hanlon had spent his first day in the field watching. The more experienced snake hunters moved quickly away from the recruits, knowing the terrain and the gopher holes—which actually belonged to a large kind of land tortoise—where easy catches could be made. O'Hanlon quickly discarded their lies about the snake's habit of staying in the shade to avoid the heat of the sun. The logic seemed right; the semitropical sun was raw and unmerciful. But O'Hanlon soon recognized that the cold-blooded species needed the sun to stay warm and he'd found his first catch half-curled on a gray-white slab of limestone, the sun full on its distinctive, diamond-patterned skin. By watching the others, he'd stolen the idea of a hook at the end of the pitchfork handle fashioned from a length of stiff wire. Moving slowly, he eased the wire under the snake as it rattled its tail at him and then lifted it off the rock. By suspending the beast in air he robbed it of a solid foundation from which to launch a strike. Then, while carefully watching the movement of the head, he stuffed it into the open gunnysack and earned his first legitimate fifty cents since arriving in Florida.

By the third day he had snared ten of the animals, as many as even the more experienced men of the dozen who stayed on. At noontime old Pete fed them all lunch under any nearby shade oak. From the bed of his truck he handed out day-old loaves of hard bread, chunks of cheese cut from huge disks and all the oranges a man could eat. It was during the breaks that O'Hanlon heard that Pete collected one dollar from the land developer for each of the snakes they all caught. The old man tallied the number on his own count, though he did offer the sacks to the rich owner to count for himself. Several of the men smiled knowingly when one suggested that Pete was not beyond overstating the catch or releasing a few of the undamaged snakes to be caught and paid for again.

"That ole rich man, he'll stick his hand down your pocket to take ya'll money but he ain't gone take a chance puttin' his finger on that snake for countin'," said one, raising smiles and nods from the others.

"He don't have to when he has fools like us to do it for him," said another.

That statement put a damp silence over the

group. But when the foreman called them up they all still stretched out their legs and took to the field. O'Hanlon rose with them, the five dollars he'd earned tucked deep under the leather of his boot.

O'Hanlon kept his head down, eyes up at the brim of his hat, watching and assessing the arrival of the now close vehicles as they jounced across the open field through the brush. Within minutes he recognized the cough and clatter of old Pete's truck, but not the cream-colored touring car. He did not look up fully until they stopped ten yards away, next to an outcropping of cabbage palms. Pete's foreman, the man they called McGahee, was driving the truck and got out first, his hands in his pockets and his porkpie hat tipped back.

"Any luck, Irish?"

"Just the one so far," O'Hanlon answered, raising the bag ever so slightly.

But O'Hanlon's eyes were on the Pierce-Arrow convertible, the Florida sun flashing off its chrome and somehow melting into the glowing enamel of its polished hood. The driver got out. O'Hanlon measured him at just over six feet and 190 pounds, which he carried well. He was wearing the same shoes as the binder boys but his were new and polished. His dark suit was equally new but made of a rough cloth, and he unbuttoned his jacket as he assessed O'Hanlon from a distance. Their eyes met and neither looked away until the passenger of the car stood up in the back seat and the driver turned to open the door.

The colonel was dressed in a white linen suit complete with a vest stretched tight across his substantial belly and a straw boater with a yellow and black ribbon. He did not move to step out but instead stood erect, surveying the land from a height, his large head turning slowly. The sun made the cloth of his suit seem luminous and he raised a large cigar to his lips and posed as if he knew it.

"How is the drainage here, Mr. Pete," he said as the snakeman walked round the back of his truck.

"She's pretty dry here 'cause of the ridge, Colonel. Even in the rainy season she'll drain without too much help."

The colonel did not answer and the rest could only stand and wait. The only sound was the ticking of the cooling engines. "Too damn hot for horses in October," the colonel finally said, and moved to the doorway, which his driver now opened. On the ground his height was diminished but O'Hanlon noted that the man carried his girth with considerable grace. A starched collar pinched at the folds of flesh in his neck and a carefully trimmed walrus mus-

tache gave him a look of old English. He seemed
to be studying the sandy soil with the toe of his
polished boot; then he stepped forward to
where O'Hanlon was standing.

"How many snakes do you see a day out here,
son?"

O'Hanlon looked up into the colonel's eyes
and marked their clear grayness, a pale color
that reflected nothing. His fingers were thick
and blunt at the ends, the flat, squared nails
carefully clipped and buffed. They were not the
hands of a man easily ignored.

"The number goes up, sir, when you get better at spotting them," he answered.

"I suppose that's so," the colonel said, turning
to Mr. Pete. The snakeman took his hat off and
scratched at his balding head. McGahee turned
away, shaking his.

The colonel toed the ground again and the afternoon silence enveloped them all. The tall
driver moved up next to his boss without a
word and O'Hanlon could feel the heat on his
shoulders. A single rivulet of sweat ran down
between his shoulder blades. He watched as the
colonel bent to brush a burred sticker from his
spotless pants leg. O'Hanlon was waiting for the
gentleman to speak when he heard the dry rattle. At first he thought it was coming from his
bag but quickly realized it was unmuffled and
too sharp and just to his right. The volume in-

creased and froze all five men. O'Hanlon cut his eyes to the shade of the cabbage palm and caught the movement, the angle of the snake's strike, the sound of scaled skin on rock.

The jaws of the rattler were less than a foot from the flesh of the colonel's outstretched arm when O'Hanlon's hand snapped out in a blur and stopped it. His fist closed just behind the snake's head and twisted the body up and away, but the momentum of the animal caused its tail to snap against the colonel's pants leg. At the exact same moment an explosion sounded from O'Hanlon's left. His eyes blinked at the sound of the report but then refocused just as the snake's head disintegrated.

For a moment, all five men could only stare. O'Hanlon first looked at the shredded gristle in his fist and the blood spattering across his arm. Then he turned to see the smoking barrel of a handgun held by the colonel's driver. The tall man's arm was still locked at the elbow, his eye still sighting down the weapon. The heavy crack of the gunshot seemed to have sucked all other sound out of the air, no bird or breeze or rustle of palm fronds. Even the heat seemed to have stopped at the level around their heads, robbing them all of a single breath.

"Gotdamn, boys!" Mr. Pete finally said, breaking the silence.

The colonel stood, looking first at the red knot

in O'Hanlon's hand and then at his driver's .45. He cleared his substantial throat and placed two fingers into his right ear but could only reiterate the old snakeman's reaction.

"Goddamn, gentlemen."

O'Hanlon put the palm of his hand over the tureen of soup, guarding it each time a car or truck rolled down the city street, raising a yellow film of dust that would drift with the ocean breeze and threaten his meal. He had splurged and spent twelve cents on the large pail, the extra for the chunks of beef stirred in. It was the first time he'd eaten meat since he'd come south. It was, he guessed, a celebration of sorts. He was sharing the soup with the shoeshine boy in front of his hotel, sitting up in the customer's chair while the black boy, whose name he did not know, squatted on his box.

"Colonel Bradford just give you a job," the shoeshine said again, repeating the line, and then putting another spoonful into his mouth, savoring both the taste and the idea.

After the gunshot and the cussing, the colonel had relighted his cigar and taken a more careful measure of O'Hanlon, assessing him as one might a prospective horse purchase. He was only a couple of inches shorter than the colonel's driver and several pounds lighter, though it was difficult to gauge with the ropy muscle of his forearms and the wide, coat-hanger look of his shoulders. His dark hair and nearly black eyes only gave a suggestion of immigrant. The colonel noted O'Hanlon's hands, one still loosely gripping the neck of the burlap bag, the other, blood-spattered, holding what was left of the snake. Neither of them showed even the slightest flutter.

"I could use a handsome young man up at the club," the colonel suddenly announced, turning his big head slightly to Mr. Pete's direction.

The snakeman stepped up and looked at O'Hanlon, winking as he did.

"He's the best man I got out here, Colonel. You seen how quick he is. Be a shame to lose him."

The colonel let a grin come into his face.

"I'm sure he is, Mr. Pete. But I will pay him twenty-five dollars a week and he won't have to stand out in this godforsaken sun all day." He brought a card out from his vest pocket and handed it to O'Hanlon before turning to climb back into his car. "Be at this address day after tomorrow, son. Seven a.m. sharp."

O'Hanlon finished out the day with Mr. Pete. He was paid for three more snakes caught before twilight and his pay included fifty cents for the rattler missing its head. When Pete dropped the crew of men off on the street corner at dusk, he caught O'Hanlon's attention and called him to the opened window of the truck. He lowered his voice even though their faces were drawn near.

"You got somethin' in your eye, boy, though I cain't say what," the old man said, trying to look under the brim of O'Hanlon's hat. "You best think on it hard when you're up to the colonel's, 'cause if you're 'spectin' to outsmart somebody for they money with that quick hand and brain of yours, that ain't the place to do it. Ain't nobody took nothin' off the colonel and walked away with it."

O'Hanlon tilted his head up from the shadow of its brim, exposing a bemused look on his face. He squinted into the old man's eyes, challenged by the thought that they might hold the same power to glimpse a man's soul as his own.

"Thank you, sir," he finally said, the first time in the days he'd spent with the old man that he'd spoken directly to him. "I will appreciate the advice, sir, I'm sure."

Danny O'Hanlon's father didn't need to tell his son that he would never make it as a fighter. He knew himself by the time he was seventeen that his near-photographic memory of technique and tactics, his ability at assessing an opponent and the undeniable quickness of his hands and feet were not enough. He could pound the heavy bag for hours, rattle the speed bag until it sang like a snare drum and work endlessly in the ring with a seemingly limitless endurance. But the desire was missing. He was not like the desperate ones who melded hunger and meanness together with a physical talent to satisfy both. He had done well in amateur bouts, but when he worked the corners with his father at the professional matches he could see the hearts in men who knew and wanted nothing more than the fight. He also saw the men with money in the third row, watching intently, not guffawing or shaking their fists in elation or rage, but watching. The rich got richer without pain. They only watched, while the fighters let their hearts bleed.

"It's off limits, son," his father would say when he caught Danny staring at the fine suits and glossy women in row three. "They're born to it, lad; forget about it." And Danny O'Hanlon would turn back to watch men at war, but he would not forget. On his twentieth birthday he left New York, left this father's corner as the cut man and took the train south. Now he'd met a rich man, and seen his eyes and hands.

"I got me a cousin works the Breakers Hotel up to Palm Beach," said the shoeshine, still working his soup. "Been tryin' to get me a job in that place almost a year now. Says that's where all the rich folk are."

O'Hanlon knew of the talk. The railroad and

tourist hotel Henry Flagler built on the island of Palm Beach was well known. He had overheard locker-room talk by fighters and their hangers-on who knew when certain people left the city and "the dollars went south for the winter."

Both he and the shoeshine boy had gone quiet with the thought of it, both looking out into the growing twilight, chewing softly on the bits of beef and their own image of money.

"My cousin says the colonel own the finest gamblin' joint in Florida, right there on Palm Beach island," said the shoeshine.

"I thought gambling was illegal in Florida," O'Hanlon said, though he'd seen plenty of it since his arrival.

"Hell, Irish. Ain't nothin' illegal you got that kind of money. My cousin say one a his favorite customers go to the colonel's every night but Sunday when he in the Poinciana Hotel. Get his shoes all shined every single time like a routine and give my cousin a silver dollar. Says it's lucky. You believe that, Irish?"

O'Hanlon scraped up the final spoonful of soup, the sound of metal on metal making a soft, screeching sound.

"How would I know about lucky?"

"What you mean, 'How would you know'? You got you a job wit' the colonel, Irish! You done got you some lucky."

* * *

That night O'Hanlon swam in the ocean again. He took a bus to A1A and made his way down to the beach well past dark. It was a windless night and the small breakers made only a hissing sound when they washed up and for a moment made a new dark border in the sand. He stripped to his shorts and eased himself step by step into the black water up to his shoulders and then turned to mark a beachfront light as a bearing. The current was pulling softly north and he began stroking straight out, a metronome in his head, a beat built with routine. Every three hundred strokes he would stop and turn, treading water long enough to find the high beach light and then adjust his course. His muscles were tight in the first two sets but then loosened with the action. The taste of salt water in his mouth again reminded him of summers on Coney Island, his father frantic with his six-year-old son's ludicrous ability to swim in the Atlantic without a single lesson or practice. After ten three-hundred-stroke turns, the light had disappeared in the distance, and O'Hanlon kept on. He had heard once from a lifeguard on Coney Island that no man would swim too far out in the ocean to get back, simply because he would have no choice but to get back. At the twenty-first turn O'Hanlon stopped swimming and flipped over on his back, his lungs aching, his eyes looking up at a black bowl of stars.

There was nothing to hear but the beat of his heart in his ears. Nothing to feel but the gentle movement of the swells, raising him first, only inches, and then settling him back. He never thought of what was below the surface. Never let his imagination hold sharks or hungry blue fish eyeing his floating white flesh. Out here he could just drift and focus and plan. With his ears in the water he could track out a plan in the stars and let it roll or start it all over again until he could see it. Then, when the vision was clear, he would turn to land and begin stroking again, watching for the light, timing his endurance until he would finally stagger back up the sand, confident that he could make it again.

The eastern sky was still dusky gray when the train slowed for the West Palm Beach station. O'Hanlon timed an oncoming patch of dark brush and jumped. He let his knees take the shock of the landing and rolled onto one shoulder, his arms wrapped around the waterproof canvas bag stuffed with all his possessions.

He waited in the groundcover, the smell of cinder and dry grass in his nose. No shouts or whistles, only the same clack of metal and shiver of hinged wood that had drowned out his noise when he'd jumped the freight car after midnight back in Miami. In time he gained his feet and moved away toward the streets, brushing the dirt and sticker seeds from his pants legs. At first he used the alleys and the walls of wooden storage shacks and warehouses for cover until he was several blocks to the east. Only then did he step out into the wide expanse of a city street and try to take his bearings.

The shoeshine had given him directions, told him to look for the tall, white-stucco building rising above town and use it as a landmark. From that tower the bridge across the lake would be due east. It was the shoeshine who also convinced O'Hanlon to jump the night train north.

"Ya'll still gonna have some walkin' to do. Best get there early, Irish. Ya'll don't want ta keep the Colonel waitin'."

O'Hanlon kept moving east toward a lightening sky. The street was lined with small cottages set back off the roadway, the lean of their rooflines their only distinction. An occasional lantern light could be seen coming through a window. Working people, up in the predawn to start their day. Farther on, the working-class houses were replaced by small shop fronts and automobile repair bays, and then the paved streets of a true business section began. A milk delivery truck passed him. A man dressed in a suit coat walked a dog. Along the way O'Hanlon noted the same interruption in construction that he'd seen in Miami. Lots with foundations already set, but unfinished walls left ragged. Piles of fill dirt were sprouting weeds from sitting too long undisturbed. They were projects started and then abruptly stopped by worried investors. By the time he reached the lakefront, the top five floors of the ten-story building were glowing in the early rays of sunrise. It was the only thing that seemed beyond pedestrian on this side of the lake. But on the opposite shore, even in the early shadows, O'Hanlon could see Henry Flagler's Royal Poinciana Hotel, stretched out in white like some languorous, highly bred woman. Even from here one could see the distinction. Even from here one knew where the clean ocean breezes stopped first. On the island was where the untroubled money was.

The tender at the western end of the bridge took a full minute to judge O'Hanlon before allowing him to pass, the man's rheumy eyes jumping from the colonel's card to O'Hanlon's face and clothes and the bag he carried.

"Working for the colonel, eh?"

O'Hanlon nodded. The tender looked once more at the bag and then tipped his head to the east.

"Just north of the hotel, son. And nowhere else."

O'Hanlon retrieved the card and started his walk, counting his steps over the length of the span, looking down into the clear water, judging its depth and the pull of its currents.

By the time he reached the eastern end the sun was streaming through the fronds of the few planted palm trees and his shirt was pasted to his back with an early sweat.

Carpets of thick leafed grass and a military-like line of royal palms banked the lane that led past the hotel to the colonel's. O'Hanlon could see glimpses of the new mansions set back off the roadway and done in the Mediterranean revival style of white-stucco arches and terra-cotta tiles.

The colonel's was more modest. It was a white-framed, two-story affair on the lakefront with striped canvas overhangs and a pyramid-shaped shingled roof at the entrance. Several louvered cupolas were situated on the shingled roof to vent the heat. On the street side a five-foot-tall cement wall guarded the front of the club. There was no movement at the front so O'Hanlon followed the sound of a truck engine and voices around to a side alley and approached a group of three men unloading cases of fresh produce and cartons of dry goods. He was about to ask for the colonel when the driver's voice sounded from a porch above.

"Well, if it isn't snake boy come to work an honest day."

O'Hanlon looked up to see the man he would

now always consider "the gunman" in his internal file of new faces and then back to the workers. Their heads had snapped up at the sound of the voice but then quickly turned back to their lifting and carrying once they knew it was not their duty to respond.

"I came for the colonel," O'Hanlon said.

"No. You came to work, snake boy. So quit standing around and work," the gunman said. "Next wagon's comin' round the corner, boys. Let's get to it."

O'Hanlon dropped his bag near the picket fence and joined the brigade line, passing food cartons and cases of illegal liquor hand to hand in through the kitchen door. No one said a word to him. The occasional grunts and exhalations of the men remained the only sound as the sun rose, the alley warmed and the next truck pulled in.

O'Hanlon spent his first three days working the trucks, digging out rooted palms on the property and replanting tropical ferns. At night he would walk back over the bridge where he'd found a cheap room with the other workers. After a week he'd figured out that the driver, who'd become Mr. Brasher, was also the security captain of sorts. The four quiet men who reported to the house after dinnertime dressed in plain black suits gave deferential nods to the workers and then disappeared into the building, only to be seen later, walking the upstairs porches or peering from high railings. Another man stayed close to Brasher at all times, agreeing when spoken to, occasionally scratching down an instruction on a small pad.

One morning O'Hanlon and the work crew were breaking up a coral outcrop to run a waterline to the main house when a slab of rock slipped from its lashings and fell from the back of a truck. The sharp coral sliced through the lower leg of an older worker called Mauricio, crushing his ankle. His scream brought Brasher and his assistant running from the house. When the group lifted away the boulder, Mauricio's leather boot lay at a sickening right angle to his leg. While the others simply stared, O'Hanlon quickly went to work, carefully ripping away the man's blood-soaked trouser. The glisten of wet, white bone shown through the cleaved and reddening meat of muscle. Brasher's assistant, a man called Dimmett, drew a sharp breath and even Brasher took a slight step back. O'Hanlon checked their reactions and then used his left hand to squeeze shut the fleshy wound, and as blood flowed between his fingers he called out for supplies.

"Towels! Clean towels!" he yelled at no one in particular, but it was one of his crew that went running.

"Do you have a first-aid kit?" he said, this

time looking up to Brasher, who seemed to be confused by the question. "Some bandages? Some iodine? You don't want this getting infected, boss. It's way too deep for that."

Brasher shook his head, then looked up to the porch where one of his men was standing, the metal barrel of a rifle in his hands, watching the commotion.

"In the casino!" Brasher called up to him. "Get that first-aid pouch from behind the coat-check counter." The man hurried off. The laborer scrambled back with an armload of kitchen towels and O'Hanlon pressed one flat to the wound and wrapped it with another.

"I need your belt, boss," O'Hanlon said. Brasher's hand went to his buckle but stopped. He looked at Dimmett and flicked a finger. The other security man pulled his belt off and had to grab at the Colt revolver that he carried in a holster at the small of his back. O'Hanlon watched the man fumble with the weapon and then took the belt and tied it tight around the reddening wrap of towels. He looked into Mauricio's eyes and watched the pupils dilate and roll with oncoming shock.

"Let's get him over to the doc's at the hotel," O'Hanlon said, looking up at Brasher, who hesitated. "Come on!" he said. "If that artery in his calf is split, he's going to lose a lot of blood."

Brasher looked down again at the towels.

"You'll have to take him over the bridge. There's a doctor's right on Clematis by the drugstore."

"Brasher, the doc from the hotel was here in five minutes last night when that lady fainted inside," O'Hanlon said. "Hell, it'll take us near thirty to bounce him over to West Palm."

The other laborers didn't look up to see Brasher's face and instead moved to lay the rest of the towels as a mat in the bed of the truck.

"Then you better get moving, snake boy," Brasher said, and motioned the other security man to help gather up Mauricio. "The help don't get treated at the hotel."

O'Hanlon held Brasher's eyes longer than he wanted to, then moved to Mauricio's legs while the others hooked under his arms. Once they had him settled in the truck Dimmett climbed in to drive and O'Hanlon watched through the back window as the security man carelessly put the handgun on the seat beside him.

It was after five when they returned from the mainland. Brasher was waiting.

"Colonel wants you out front, parking cars," he said, handing O'Hanlon a suit complete with new shoes. "You do know how to drive?"

"Not a problem," O'Hanlon said.

"Good. Get cleaned up and get something to eat and be out on the front porch at seven."

Throughout the night he politely greeted the colonel's guests, ladies in fine summer fashions, men in dark, conservative suits. The autos were all expensive sedans and touring cars. They all smelled of fine perfume and hair tonic. O'Hanlon only ground the gears of one, for which he received a smirk from the other valets.

When the evening was through, the colonel, with Brasher two steps behind, escorted the last of the guests to the street. O'Hanlon was sent scurrying for the car and returned with the Collingsworths' Chrysler B70. The colonel held the passenger door for the lady and O'Hanlon the driver's side for Mr. Collingsworth. When the car rumbled off, the colonel, dressed in a tuxedo, waited until O'Hanlon gained the sidewalk before speaking.

"I understand you may have saved a man's leg today Mr., uh—"

"O'Hanlon, sir. Danny O'Hanlon."

"Irish?"

"Yes, sir."

"From New York City?"

"Chicago," O'Hanlon lied, cutting his eyes to Brasher.

"You're too young to have been in the war. Where did you learn your medical skills?"

"My father, sir. I was a corner man with my father in the fight game," O'Hanlon said, going back to the truth.

"Fight game," said the colonel, the taste of disapproval on his voice. He took a draw from his Cuban cigar. "A nasty business."

O'Hanlon said nothing. Then the colonel extended his arm and slipped a ten dollar bill into his hand. He stared at the bill a moment, unsure what the philanthropy might cost him.

"Thank you, sir."

"You earned it, lad. Report here for the rest of the week. Mr. Brasher will look after you."

The colonel took another deep draw of smoke and looked up through the palm fronds at a waxing moon.

"Another beautiful night in paradise," he said, perhaps to himself. "But duty calls. Let us do the count and see how much they left behind tonight."

O'Hanlon stood unmoving but caught Brasher's final look as he held the door for the colonel and then shut it. The distinct snap of a metal lock sounded. Only then did he leave, heading south to the bridge and then walking its span, watching the water and marking the lights of the West Palm high-rise in the distance.

It was another week before he saw the inside of the casino itself. An arriving guest had bashed into the rear bumper of another guest's automobile. The valet behind the wheel of the damaged car said he did not recall the name of the owner.

O'Hanlon's perfect memory had "Mr. Reed" instantly on his tongue and Brasher sent him inside to give the news to the man. Inside he approached a man he knew to be the floor manager.

Reed was pointed out, standing at one of the English hazard tables. The room was tastefully decorated; brocaded sofas, tall-stemmed lamps and polished wood. Around the roulette, faro and other gaming tables the men stood exchanging polite conversation. They seemed to be only mildly distracted by the play of the cards or the spin of the wheel, and when they became too animated, their wives' faces turned chilly with reproach. O'Hanlon had not expected the kind of raucous backslapping and cussing he'd been a part of in locker-room poker games, but the quiet, controlled atmosphere unsettled him at first. His discomfort subsided as he moved through the room, working his way to the side of Mr. Reed, and he realized that no one seemed to notice him, or if they did, they were trying mightily to ignore his presence. When he got to Reed's elbow he stood for a few extra seconds, watching the route of money moving from tables to drawers. He scanned the room for office doors or the presence of the quiet security men he knew were somewhere on duty. Then he excused himself and sought Reed's attention. The man turned to him and listened to the message and then dismissed O'Hanlon with a wave of limp fingers as if an errant mosquito had pestered him. "Park it, boy. We'll see to it tomorrow."

O'Hanlon kept his hands clasped behind his back, nodded, and in a low voice said, "She's a beauty, sir. We're very sorry."

Reed looked at him again, this time with more interest. "And she will be again, son. With a bit of luck," he said, turning back to his game.

O'Hanlon excused himself and walked away, again taking in the layout, the length of hallways and the single staircase in view. "Bit of luck," he whispered to himself.

He picked a particularly busy Friday night, one with a clear sky and no moon. An easy southeasterly breeze was blowing in from the Atlantic. He'd counted and timed the retiring guests so that the final car was his to fetch. The others were gone when he returned with the car and the front of the club went quiet as it pulled away. O'Hanlon waited several minutes at the wall, giving the colonel and Brasher time to gather the money from the drawers and retire to the colonel's office to count it. While he waited he picked the lock on the front door and then stepped back out to see Dimmett making his final rounds on the balcony. The security man would be in the hallway in between thirty and thirty-five seconds at O'Hanlon's count, like every night before. Under the lamplight O'Hanlon extracted a flask and poured a pint of pig's blood that he'd bottled from a West Palm butcher shop onto his pants leg from the thigh down, smeared the thick red fluid with his hands and added a smear across his cheek.

At his count of twenty-eight he staggered into the hallway and cut his eyes to the top of the stairs where Dimmett's footsteps were just falling. He groaned and stumbled into the bottom two risers and heard the security man catch his breath and say, "Christ!"

"Hit! By the B70," O'Hanlon spat out between his teeth, clutching his leg with both hands, the blood oozing between his fingers. Dimmett bent and started to reach down but recoiled at the sight and froze.

"Your belt, man! It's a cut artery," O'Hanlon hissed through his teeth, urgent but not too loud. Dimmett was panicky. He undid his buckle, stripped the belt out and ignored the sound of the revolver as it tumbled onto the wooden step behind him. When he bent forward to wrap the belt around the leg, O'Hanlon arched back, picked up the Colt and came down hard on the back of Dimmett's skull with the butt. He cradled the unconscious body and waited a full minute, listening. The club remained silent. His first assessment? True to form.

Gaining his feet, O'Hanlon put the Colt in his waistband at the small of his back and then slung Dimmett's arm over his shoulder and hefted him. He now knew the way down the hall to the colonel's office. With the security man propped up against the doorframe, he banged the oak door with the heel of his hand, hoping to move the people inside but not arouse others still in the club. He heard footsteps and then Brasher's voice.

"Who is it?"

"It's Dimmett," said O'Hanlon. "He's been hit by a car."

"O'Hanlon? You know the damn rules, O'Hanlon. Nobody's allowed in here after closing."

"Christ, Brasher! The man's hurt bad. It was a customer who hit him for Christ's sake!"

O'Hanlon heard the colonel's muffled baritone voice, too soft to make out the words. A metal lock snapped open from the inside. Brasher opened the door a few inches and looked squarely into Dimmett's slack face and then at O'Hanlon's blood-smeared cheek. "The hell?" Brasher said, letting the door swing wider.

O'Hanlon timed the movement, like a good fighter using his opponent's own body momentum to set him up. When Brasher stepped back, O'Hanlon pushed Dimmett's dead

weight up and into Brasher's left hand, which
was already holding the .45. Brasher hooked
his gun arm under the falling man to support
him and O'Hanlon instantly snapped down on
the barrel of the gun, twisting it up against the
falling weight of Dimmett's body. A muffled
snap sounded as Brasher's trigger finger broke
at the knuckle and by the time his knee hit the
floor O'Hanlon had the .45 pointed at his face
while the Colt in his other hand was trained
across the room on the colonel's chest. Both of
the men froze.

"Well, goddamn, gentlemen," O'Hanlon said
quietly. "This—is a robbery."

With the .45 at the colonel's temple, it took
only five minutes for Brasher to tie both his em-
ployer and Dimmett with lengths of wet
rawhide O'Hanlon had brought with him in his
waterproof bag. O'Hanlon only let the colonel
call him a common thief and a fool once before
gagging the old man with a satin handkerchief
from his own suit pocket. There was no comment from Brasher, only a smoldering, animal
stare as O'Hanlon finally lashed him to a fine
and sturdy straight-backed chair.

The office safe behind the colonel's desk had
not yet been opened, or had perhaps been
slammed shut at the initial knock on the door.
But O'Hanlon was not a greedy man. The three
hundred thousand dollars in cash still in par-

tially counted stacks on the colonel's desk was enough. He pushed the bills into his waterproof bag and closed it.

"Nobody steals from the colonel and gets away with it. We'll hunt you down, snake boy," Brasher finally said.

O'Hanlon shook his head, gagged Brasher and then moved to the door and listened for any movement out in the hall.

"Tough to find much cooperation with the law when you explain that the stolen cash came from an illegal gambling operation?" he said, leaving the rhetorical question in the air. "Snake eyes, Brasher. It's all a gamble."

O'Hanlon could hear the scrape of the chair the second he closed the door. He knew the route through the club to the back and marched out, moving fast, but not running. At the open kitchen door he saw the chef, carving at something on the counter, and two of the security men on the other side, waiting for the food. He ducked by without being seen, crossed the slate patio outside and slipped into the dense wall of palm fronds and sea grape leaves to the rear gate. Sharp voices and a scuffling of feet sounded as he latched the door and headed into a neighbor's yard. Floodlights came on behind him and he moved into the alley. He did not look back, did not panic, and never stopped moving east until he felt water.

He could feel the body of the swells below him, rising and falling, working against him, but not hard enough. He kept a rhythm with his feet, flutter kicking at a pace he could keep forever. On the darkened beach, O'Hanlon had filled two bicycle tires and positioned them inside the bag and next to the money. He tucked his clothes inside, then sealed the duffel shut and pushed off onto the sea. That was the beauty of the island, the security that the rich felt knowing they were on an island with only one entrance across the bridge. The better to keep the riffraff away. O'Hanlon knew Brasher would shut that route first. He knew he'd work the lake shorelines. Maybe they would get to the beach, figure out the ocean escape eventually. But the flow from the southeast would keep him moving up the coast. He could make three or four miles by sunup.

When he finished his third three-hundred-stroke turn he rolled over and hooked his arms over the bag. His muscles were warm from the work. The taste of salt water was in his mouth again and he watched the lights of the Breakers Hotel on the beach disappear in the distance. There was nothing to hear but the beat of his heart in his ears. Nothing to feel but the gentle movement of the swells, raising him first, only inches, and then settling him back. In the stars he tracked a plan, and when the vision was clear, he would turn to land and begin stroking. No man goes out too far to make it back, simply because he has no other choice.

Henry and the Idiots

Robert J. Randisi

Bob Randisi has chronicled the lives and times of PIs Miles Jacoby and Nick Delvecchio over the years. Presently he is describing the life experiences of a police detective named Joe Keough, in novels such as 2002's *East of the Arch* (St. Martin's Press) and the upcoming *Arch Angels* (SMP, 2003). Here he tells a tale of the way a sudden gambling windfall can affect the lives of more than just the big winner. His venue shifts from Midwest Mississippi riverboats cross country to Reno, Nevada, and gambling points in between.

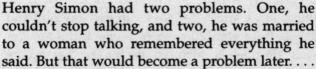

1

Henry Simon had two problems. One, he couldn't stop talking, and two, he was married to a woman who remembered everything he said. But that would become a problem later. . . .

Most jackpots come when you're not looking. This one was no different. Henry Simon was ogling another of the casino's waitresses as she went by, her ass twitching, both cheeks just about hanging out of her outfit, when the card he needed for a royal flush in Caribbean stud poker fell. The jackpot payoff was two hundred and fifty-seven thousand dollars and change. No one had hit it in quite some time.

This was on the *Casino Queen* across the Mississippi in East St. Louis. Henry actually lived in St. Louis with his wife and her two idiot brothers. That was what he called them, the idiots—

only he didn't say it out loud because Mildred was the only one who could insult her idiot brothers.

Anyway, he usually went gambling with Mildred, and they usually went to the President Casino on the *Admiral,* which was docked on the St. Louis side of the river. On this night Henry felt like gambling, and Mildred didn't, so he went alone with her words echoing in his ears.

"You ain't gonna win nothin'!" she shouted at him. "You never win when you go without me."

.Well, that may or may not have been true, but it certainly wasn't on this night. Henry had hit the jackpot, and when they came to pay him and asked if he wanted cash or a check the answer was simple—he wanted cash. The reason he wanted cash was because he was going to leave the casino with the money, get in his car and start driving AWAY from St. Louis. He would not Pass Go, he would not Collect Two Hundred Dollars, because he had won over two hundred and fifty thousand dollars and neither Mildred nor her idiot brothers were going to see a dime of it. . . .

"Because," he told his new friend, who was sitting next to him in a Sparks, Nevada, keno parlor in John Ascuaga's Nugget Hotel & Casino, "I always swore that if I ever hit it big,

I'd get in the car and keep driving and not look back."

"So you just left your wife behind?" the man asked.

"Mister—what's yer name?"

"Oh, I'm Al," the man said, "Al Manning."

"Henry's my name," Henry said, and the two shook hands. "Well, Al, let me tell ya, I not only left my wife behind, I left her two idiot brothers, I left my job—hell, man, I left my life behind— that life, anyway. I'm on to a new one, now."

"But . . . doesn't she wonder where you are?"

"I guess she does," Henry said. "We been married like twenty years, so I guess when I didn't come home the next mornin' she probably wondered."

"And that doesn't bother you?"

"Naw," Henry said, keeping his eyes on the numbers that were now being flashed on the red keno board in front of them. "See, Mildred's a grade A bitch. I'd 'a left her a long time ago if I had the money—or the balls. See, when you win a ton of money, ya suddenly got balls, too."

"I guess so," the man said. He shook his head when the numbers stopped flashing and tore up one of the tickets he was holding. "How much did you win again?"

"Over two hundred and fifty thousand," Henry said.

"And you just . . . left."

"I went out into the parking lot, got into my car and drove to Kansas City . . ."

In Kansas City Henry stopped at the huge Ameristar Casino Hotel complex, parked, went inside and got a room without asking how much it was. It had taken him six hours to get from St. Louis to Kansas City, because he had stopped at the Isle of Capri Casino in Boonville on the way. He'd always wanted to go there since it opened a couple of years ago, but Mildred had always said, "Why ya wanna go drivin' hours to a casino when we got four of 'em right here?"

Mildred never wanted to go anywhere. Ever since he'd taken her out of a trailer in Dupo, Illinois, and married her they hadn't gone anywhere, not even to the Mecca of gambling cities, Las Vegas. It had always been Henry's dream to go to Las Vegas, but his dreams meant nothing to a woman who had none of her own. So he was stuck in his house in Dogtown with Mildred and the two idiots, working his job at the brewery and going to the boats whenever he could. He never gave up his dreams, though. He knew that if he ever hit it big, he was gonna go everywhere he ever wanted to go, and he started with Boonville, Missouri.

He stopped at the casino, played some table games and machines for a while, then ate in the great delicatessen they had there. They even gave you cash back the same day for the time you played, so he ended up eating for nothing—even though he could have afforded to eat in their steakhouse with no problem.

He left the Isle of Capri a couple of hundred of his money, but that didn't bother him none, not when he was sitting on two hundred and fifty K.

He had made one stop along the way in a Kmart to buy a money belt and a fanny pack. He'd had the casino pay him in fifties and hundreds, so he stuffed most of that into the money belt and then put about ten grand in the fanny pack. He hated fanny packs, but with it around his waist nobody noticed he was also bulging from a stuffed money belt.

So he'd taken a couple of hundred out of the fanny pack and gambled it at the Isle of Capri, then he ate and got back on the road.

He'd hit his big jackpot right at the end of the night, buying his chips with his last fifty bucks, so by the time he got paid and was escorted to the parking lot by a security guard he magnanimously tipped a hundred bucks, it was six a.m. When he walked into his room at the Ameristar Casino in K.C. it was after noon, and he was pooped. He decided to sack out for a while before deciding what to do next. He knew he wasn't going to stay in Kansas City, but they had three casinos—which, like all Missouri casinos, were technically "boats," because they were on or near water—a horse track and a dog track, so he was going to spend some time at each before continuing on. He just didn't know yet where he'd be continuing on to. He was going to decide that later. . . .

"Weren't you afraid your wife and her brothers would find you?" Al asked.

"Not in Kansas City," Henry said. "In fact, I don't know where Mildred would look for me, or if she even would. Maybe she'd say good riddance. I didn't know, and I didn't care, and I still don't."

He paused so they could both watch the numbers come up on the green Keno board, and in spite of himself he wondered what Mildred's reaction had been when he didn't show up home. . . .

2

"That stupid sonofabitch didn't come home last night," Mildred raged at her two brothers as they spooned Fruit Loops into their mouths. She had marveled for years at how most of the milk would spill off their spoons and down their chins with every bite. What the hell was so hard about finding your mouth with a goddamned spoon?

"Wha' happen' ta him?" one of them asked

with his mouth full. He was Brother, her oldest brother.

"I don't know what happened to him, god-damn it, that's what I'm tellin' you." She stood over them in her housedress, hair frizzed out in every direction, looking for all the world like their mother did for years, except without the hair curlers. She knew she resembled her mother and didn't mind a bit. That woman was a saint, putting up first with a loser of a husband and then two stupid sons. When she died, leav-ing the three of them in that trailer in Dupo, it fell to Mildred to care for them, even though they were both older than her. Now she was in her thirties, they were in their forties, and for the most part they still acted like they were teenagers. Give them credit, though, when it came right down to it they did what she told them to.

"I want you both to go out and find him and bring him home."

"Where is he?" brother number two, Sonny, asked.

"Fuck, ain't you listenin'?" she railed. "If I knew where he was I wouldn't be tellin' you two ta go out and find him, would I?"

Brother finished his cereal, gulped his juice and then asked, "Where do we start?"

"Start at the boat," she said, "he went gam-bling on the boat last night."

"Without you?" Sonny asked, with the last of his milk on his chin. "He don't never win nothin' without you."

"I know that," she said, "but maybe the fool actually did win a couple of hundred bucks and got hit on the head or somethin'. Go down to the *Admiral* and ask around."

The two idiots stared at each other.

"Go now!" she shouted, and they both leaped out of their chairs and fled from the room.

Henry may have been a loser like her old man, but he was her loser. Besides, if he'd stayed out drinkin' or actually found a woman who'd let him sleep with her, she'd have his ass in a sling!

When her brothers returned later that day she demanded to know where Henry was.

"We didn't find him, Milly," Brother said.

"Why the hell not?"

"Nobody at the boat saw him," Sonny said.

"But the folks at the boat now wasn't there last night," Brother added.

"Well, then, go on back and wait for them folks who was there last night," she said. "Find somebody who saw him there!"

"Can we gamble while we're there, sis?" Sonny asked.

"You got money?"

"Some."

"Go ahead and gamble it, then," she said,

"but you ain't gonna win without me, you know."

"It'll pass the time," Brother said. "Come on, Sonny."

As the boys left, Mildred shook her head, wondering if something had happened to her husband. There was always a chance maybe he did win something, and somebody robbed him. He could be floating out there in the Mississippi, the stupid jerk. She told him not to go gambling without her.

If he was alive the boys'd bring him back. If he was dead . . . well, if he wasn't dead, she'd make him wish he was.

3

"So I gambled in all three Kansas City casinos, and both tracks—dog and horse—and then you know what I did?"

"What?" Al asked. He had just come back from cashing in one of his keno tickets. He'd made twenty bucks and had reinvested it in twenty more games. So far, Henry hadn't hit his number, red or green. Most casinos ran two games at one time, differentiating by color.

"I bought me an SUV to drive the rest of the way," Henry said. "Brand-new one, red as a cherry."

"And you drove straight here?"

"Naw, not straight here," Henry said. "Tell ya what I did. . . ."

From Kansas City he drove to Council Bluffs, Iowa. There were three casinos there, too. One was Harrah's, the other Ameristar, and the third one was in Bluffs Run, the dog track, although it was now called Harrah's Bluffs Run Casino.

By the time he hit a small jackpot—ten thousand dollars—in Harrah's, he had been gone from St. Louis for five days. He was playing ten play poker, a game that allowed you to play ten hands of poker at one time. He was playing quarters, so when the machine dealt him a royal flush, the payout was a thousand dollars a hand. They had machines that dealt fifty and a hundred hands at a time, but they were mostly penny to nickel machines. He liked poker, but looking at all those little hands on the screen would have given him a headache.

As they paid him he had to laugh to himself. Once ten grand would have been a huge payout for him, but now all it did was replenish what he had lost since he left St. Louis, so he still pretty much had two hundred and fifty grand. . . .

"Poker again, huh?" Al asked, interrupting him.

"Yup."

"Seems you're pretty lucky at poker, lately. Why you playing keno, now?"

"Well, I kept trying poker, even moved on to dollar machines. I played at all three Council Bluffs casinos, never hit another thing, so I moved on. . . ."

He had to drive through Nebraska, Wyoming and Utah on Highway 80 before he came to another casino. Right at the border of Utah and Nevada he came to a town called Wendover. As he drove in he saw a population sign that stated 2,842 people lived there. The casinos included Stateline Casino and Hotel, the Peppermill, the Rainbow and the Silver Smith.

He knew that there were casinos in Nevada, but he thought it was just Vegas, Reno and Laughlin. What he didn't expect was other small towns with casinos.

He gambled at the Stateline for a while, then decided to get a room and stay in Wendover, trying the other casinos before moving on.

By this time he'd been gone from St. Louis for twelve days.

Mildred was livid. Twelve days and that sonofabitch hadn't shown up or called.

"Maybe he's dead," Brother suggested.

"He ain't dead," she said. "That sonofabitch grew some balls and left me."

"Why would he do that?" Sonny asked.

"How the hell do I know why he'd do that?" she demanded, waving her arms. "Why would he want to leave all this?"

The two brothers stared at each other, then shrugged and went back to their Cap'n Crunch. Different cereal, same milk on their chins.

She marveled at how living with her brothers while Henry was around hadn't been so bad, but with that bastard gone her brothers suddenly seemed unbearable.

She hated to admit it, but Henry was like a buffer between her and the boys. Without him, she'd probably end up killing them.

"Get dressed," she said.

"What?" Brother asked.

"Get dressed and go check the other casinos. Check the *Casino Queen*. Maybe he decided to go there. Maybe somebody will remember."

"But . . . that was twelve days ago," Sonny said.

"And check Fairmount. Maybe he decided to go to the track."

"Milly—" Brother started.

"Just do what I say, damn it!"

Both boys leaped up from the table and went to get dressed, leaving a trail of milk behind them. . . .

4

"I lost money playin' in Wendover, but there were some nice casinos there."

"I've never been there," Al said. "Been to Laughlin and Vegas, Reno and here, but none of the other places."

"Well, I left Wendover and drove on to Elko. That's even smaller than Wendover, but it still has a few casinos. Big ones, too."

"Man, you really made some stops, huh?" Al asked.

"I ain't done tellin' ya, yet. . . ."

After Wendover Henry stopped in the tiny town of Wells, which surprised him by having four casinos. In fact, he was shocked to find that the truck stop there was a casino. He gambled a while in the Lucky J's, but then moved on.

Nevada was a great state!

Henry drove into Elko in the afternoon, got himself a room right away. He had already decided that he'd get a room in any town that had more than a few casinos. He was having the time of his life and had stopped wondering about Mildred, and about the idiots, and what they were doing. All he cared about was what he was doing. And he was doing fine!

He got a room in Elko in the Red Lion Inn &

Casino, then drove around and found the Stockman's Casino and Hotel, which seemed to cater to a younger crowd. He stopped at a couple of others but spent most of his time gambling at the Red Lion. He got hot at a blackjack table, asked for the limit to be raised and then lost ten thousand dollars. They comped his room, but that was all he came away from Elko with.

After two weeks Mildred was ready to hire a private detective, since her brothers had been able to find out nothing. She was actually looking in the phone book for one when she got a call from one of her best friends, Peggy, who still lived in Dupo.

"Oh my God, oh my God!" Peggy gushed. "What are you gonna do with all that money?"

"All what money?" Mildred asked. "What the hell are you talkin' about, Peggy?"

"The money Henry won at the *Casino Queen*!"

"Are you crazy?"

"Don't tell me he didn't tell you?"

Mildred closed the phone book and paid attention.

"Peggy, what are you sayin'?"

"I was at the *Casino Queen* last night," the woman said. "Henry's picture is on the Winners' Wall."

"What?"

"He won over two hundred and fifty thousand dollars in Caribbean stud poker!"

Mildred slammed the phone down and swore with feeling. "That sonofa*bitch*!"

After leaving Elko he drove on to Winnemucca. This town of just under ten thousand people had six casinos, with three—the Red Lion, Model T and Winners—also being hotels. Since he'd liked his room in the Red Lion in Elko he decided to take one here as well and hit all six casinos. It would be a good way to celebrate two weeks on the road, and away from Mildred and the idiots.

"Sonofabitch!" Mildred swore again.

She, Sonny and Brother were standing in front of the *Casino Queen*'s Winners' Wall, staring at a photo of Henry Simon. He had a stupid grin on his face and was holding a huge, phony check. They knew the check was phony because the *Casino Queen* staff was only too happy to tell her they had paid Henry in cash.

"Our jackpot payouts are public knowledge," the man from the general manager's office said. "We announce them over the loudspeaker, and that's why we put them on this wall."

Mildred continued to glare at the photo.

"There's no problem, is there?" the man asked, worried about bad publicity.

"You tell me," she said. "My fuckin' bastard of a husband never came home after you gave him two hundred and fifty thousand dollars in cash!"

"Two hundred fifty seven thousand—" Sonny started to read from the wall, but Mildred told him savagely, "Shut up!"

"Oh, my," the man said. "I do hope nothing happened to him. He was escorted to his car by a security guard, so we know nothing happened to him *here*—"

"No," Mildred said, "nothing's happened to him. He just took off with the money is all."

"Well, uh, it's not our responsibility to make sure he, uh, went home—" the man stammered.

She turned her murderous glare on him again and he backed up, saying, "Well, if you'll excuse me . . ."

As he slunk away Brother asked, "What are we gonna do, Milly? Henry shouldn't get away with this, ya know. We coulda used some of that money."

"We?" she asked, whirling on him. "That's my damn money that motherfucking, scum-sucking, sonofabitch bastard took off with, and you better believe I'm gonna get it back!"

Sonny decided not to point out that she couldn't get back what she never had. Even his dim brain knew that wasn't the point, anyway.

"How?" Brother asked.

"His dreams, that's how."

"What?"

"Come on," she said, leading them away from the wall.

Out in the parking lot they got into Brother's white van and started back home.

"That sonofabitch was always talkin' about his fuckin' dreams," she said. "Now I'm glad I listened to him. Didn't have much choice, since he'd never shut up, anyway, but that ain't the point."

"What's the point, sis?" Sonny asked.

"Shut up and I'll tell ya! The point is, he was always mouthin' off about what he'd do if he ever hit it big. He said he'd quit his job and go live in Vegas."

"Without us?" Sonny demanded.

"Well, obviously, you stupid jerk!"

"That ain't right," Brother said. "Part of that money's rightfully our—uh, yours, sis."

"It's all mine, when I get my hands on him!" Mildred said.

"How you gonna do that?'

"You boys are gonna go and get him and bring him back here. Then I'm gonna sit down and count that money while you two kick the livin' shit outta him!"

"I can do that," Sonny said, nodding enthusiastically.

"And for every dollar that's missin' from that payout," she said, "I'm gonna have a pound of goddamn flesh!"

"But . . . how we gonna find him?" Sonny asked.

"I'll tell you how," she said, craftily. "I ain't spent years watchin' *Mannix, Barnaby Jones,* the *Rockford Files,* and *Magnum P.I.* for nothin'."

"I like *Matlock*—" Sonny started.

"Shut the fuck *up!*"

5

"I lost in Winnemucca and then I stopped in Mill City, where they only got one casino, Mr. B's. I played there for a little bit, but then I decided to head straight to Reno without any more stops."

"But here you are in Sparks," Al said. "You stopped one exit short of your goal."

"I couldn't pass this place up," Henry said. "It's huge."

The Nugget was indeed huge, with not only the keno parlor, but a sports book, race book and sixteen hundred hotel rooms.

"So I decided to stay here a couple of days before driving into Reno," Henry said. "I got in last night, got up this morning, had some breakfast and came down to the casino. For some reason I figured I'd fool around with keno for a while, and then I sat down here and met you."

"Another loser," Al said, looking up at the red screen. "You hit anything here?"

"Not a thing," Henry said, "but it's been nice talkin' to ya."

"So, Henry," Al said, as Henry stood up, "what are you going to do when you get to Reno?"

"Get a room in the biggest hotel and stay there a while," Henry said, "a long while."

Al stood up, also preparing to leave. He looked to be in his early fifties, totally bald, wearing a T-shirt and baggy shorts. Henry always had a rule against wearing shorts, but he thought that maybe since he was starting a new life, he ought to have some new rules. After all, he was about ten years younger than Al and would look better in them.

"Henry," Al said, as they shook hands, "today's my last day here. I've got to get back to work tomorrow, but let me give you one word of advice."

"What's that?"

"Don't wear that money belt in Reno."

Henry looked down at his belly quickly.

"Yeah, it shows, even wearing your shirt out," Al said.

"What do you suggest?"

"When you get to Reno, stay at the Silver

Legacy. It's one of the biggest hotels in downtown. When you get there, talk to the hotel manager, have him get the casino manager and then put your money in their safe deposit box. If you do that, they'll comp your room—as long as you gamble, that is."

"Really? I heard they comped rooms for high rollers in Vegas, but I figured that was for millionaires."

"Believe me," Al said, "you put the contents of your money belt in their vault, they'll consider you a high roller and treat you like one."

"Well, thanks for the advice, Al," Henry said. "I'm real glad I met you."

"One more piece of advice?"

"Sure," Henry said.

"Don't tell anyone else the story you just told me," the bald man said. "You might run into somebody dishonest."

"You know, I do that," Henry said. "I talk too damn much all the time. Mildred always told me that."

"You talked to your wife about your dreams?"

"Sure, who else did I have to talk to—until now?"

"So she knows what you said you'd do if you ever hit it big?"

Henry laughed. "I know what you're gettin' at, Al. I thought of that. I always told Mildred I'd

go and live in Las Vegas. If she ever goes lookin'
for me outside of Missouri, that's where she'd
look."

"I see," Al said. "Well, that was good thinking."

"I ain't as dumb as I look," Henry said to Al,
and the two men parted company, with Al
thinking, *You couldn't possibly be.*

He went up to his room to call his contact at
the Silver Legacy in Reno.

6

The Silver Legacy was a revelation to Henry.
He'd never stayed at a place so palatial, never
gambled in a place so big—and it was connected
to the Circus Circus across the street by a bridge,
and on that bridge was a snack bar, gift shop
and slot machines. The place was just amazing,
and thanks to his new friend Al, he was staying
there free.

Well, not free, exactly. He was gambling, and
after three days he had lost ten thousand dollars.
He'd tried everything. Slots, blackjack, poker of
every kind—seven card stud, Caribbean stud,
three card poker, pai gow poker, even hold'em,
which he wasn't used to playing.

But he was managing his money, like on this,
the fourth day in Reno. He woke up, had breakfast and went down to try his hand at some keno

again. Hell, his luck had gone so cold, sitting and watching keno for a while would be a good break. He only had a couple of hundred dollars left in his fanny pack, but if he could hit some numbers he wouldn't have to go into the safe deposit box again so soon. He also had a Pick 6 ticket he'd played at the Harrah's Race Book the day before that he hadn't checked on yet.

But he had no idea how cold his luck had gone until he got up to leave while his last game was counting up numbers, and he saw them. There they were, big as life—the two idiots.

He sat down again real quick, before they could see him. They were rubbernecking, looking the place over, obviously trying to find him—but *how* had they found him?

He sat hunched in his seat, hoping they'd give up and move on. Maybe they were going casino to casino. Once they left he was going to check out and get out of Reno fast. He'd have to go someplace to hide out, but he could figure that out on the road.

When he turned his head to look they were gone. He stood up cautiously, looked around and started for the elevators. Goddamn that Mildred; it had to be her who figured out where he was, because they just weren't smart enough.

He took the elevator to his floor and ran to his room. His heart was pumping now. There was no way he was going back to Missouri and Mildred. No goddamn way!

He opened his door, ran into his room and smacked right into Sonny, who slammed him against the wall. Brother was standing on the other side of the room, looking at him oddly.

"How the hell did you get in here?" he demanded.

"We slipped a few bucks to a maid, told her you was our brother and she let us in."

"How'd you know what room I was in?"

"Another few dollars to a desk clerk," Sonny said.

"You're gonna have to pay us back, though," Brother said. "We didn't have much when we got here and now we're broke. Alls we got are our return tickets."

"Sorry to hear that."

Brother was still looking at him oddly.

"Henry, how could you do a thing like this to us—to Mildred? Win all that money and take off like that. That ain't what family does."

"Family?" Henry asked. "You ain't my family, Brother."

"Mildred's your wife, and we're her brothers," Sonny said, petulantly. "If that ain't family, what is?"

"People who love each other and support each other, that's what a family is," Henry said.

"I don't get that from any of the three of you. Come on, fellas, you know what Milly's like."

"Like Momma," Sonny said, nodding his head.

"And is that a good thing?"

Sonny slammed Henry against the wall again. "What'cha sayin' about our momma?"

"Take it easy, Sonny," Brother said. "Daddy always said Momma wasn't easy to live with. I guess Milly's about the same."

"Don't let her hear you say that," Sonny warned.

"Brother, can you get this big goon to let me go?" Henry asked.

"Let him go, Sonny," Brother said. "He can't get to anywhere."

Reluctantly, Sonny released his hold on Henry.

"Stand in front of the door," Brother told him. He did so, arms folded across his chest.

"Henry," Brother said, "we got to take you back—you and the money."

"The money's gone," Henry said. "I lost it all."

"Sis said you'd lie."

"Did you search the room?" Henry asked. "Did you find any money?"

"She said you wouldn't leave it in the room. Said you'd probably put it in a . . . a safety box, or something," Sonny said.

"Safe deposit box," Brother said.

"Yeah, that was it."

Jesus, goddamn Mildred! When did she get *that* smart?

"We're gonna go downstairs and get that money," Brother said, "and then we're heading for home. Think we'll even drive there with you, maybe cash in our tickets."

"Look, boys," Henry said, "there's plenty of money. I'll give you half and you let me go. You don't even have to tell Milly about it? Tell her you couldn't find me and keep the money."

"We couldn't do that to Milly," Sonny said, then looked at Brother and asked, "Could we?"

"Shut up," Brother said. "Let's go get the money."

"I could yell for help when we get downstairs," Henry said. "Security would stop you."

"I'd hurt you, Henry," Sonny said. He was the youngest of the boys, but the biggest. "I'd have to break somethin' even before they grabbed us."

"Jesus," Henry said, shaking his head, "How'd you boys even find me?"

"That was sis's doin'," Brother said. "She said you'd probably be dumb enough to let the hotels swipe your credit cards. They led us right here."

He slapped himself in the forehead. Even though he was paying cash all the way the hotels always wanted a credit card for incidentals, like the phone and room service. They said they wouldn't swipe it, and he believed them!

"Come on, Henry," Brother said again, "let's go get the money."

7

"It was there, I swear it was," Henry said, staring at the empty safe deposit box.

Security had checked his signature, even though they'd already seen him several times over the past three days.

The idiots looked into the box over his shoulder.

"How much was there?"

"Over two hundred thousand dollars," Henry said, feeling sick.

"Jesus," Sonny said.

"Somebody stole it," Brother said.

"Duh!" Henry said.

He turned and barged out of the little room, yelling for security. . . .

"We're terribly sorry about this, Mr. Simon," the general manager of the hotel said. "Nothing like this has ever happened before."

"It only takes once," Brother said.

Henry looked up at him in wonder. It was the smartest thing he'd ever heard the man say.

"Mr. Edison?"

The head of security turned to look at the security man who had stuck his head in the door and called his name.

"What is it, Billy?"

"We, uh, got another problem, sir."

"What now?" the manager, Mr. Abraham, asked.

The security guard came into the room, which was small enough with Henry, the idiots, the general manager and the head of security in it.

"One of the guests found a, uh, dead body in the parking garage."

"What?" Abraham squawked.

"Who is it?" Tony Edison asked.

"It's Dick Jasper, sir."

"He's one of ours," Abraham said. "He's a . . . a desk clerk."

"How did he die?" Edison asked. "Heart attack?"

"No, sir," the man said. "He was murdered."

Henry looked up as the detectives came into the room. It was just him and the two of them, now. They were from the Reno PD, Detectives Hines and Dougherty. Dougherty was the strong silent type who glowered while the younger Hines did the talking.

"Well, Mr. Simon, this is what it looks like," Hines said. "The desk clerk, Jasper, must have been working with somebody. He stole the money, they must have met in the parking lot to split it and his partner killed him, stabbed him with a knife."

"Jesus," Henry said. "And my money?"

"Gone, I'm afraid."

"Oh, God!" Henry put his head in his hands. It was not so much that the money was gone as what it meant. He had to go back to Missouri and back to Mildred.

"We can tell by the hotel's computer that Jasper's the one who checked you in."

"I—I don't remember. . . ." Henry was still in a daze.

"Well, he did. Did you, uh, sign any forms with the hotel?" Hines looked at his partner. "Does the hotel insure the money kept in their boxes?"

Dougherty shrugged.

"It don't matter," Henry said. "I didn't sign nothin'."

"That is a shame," Hines said. "Well, sir, if you'll leave us an address and phone number where we can get in touch with you . . ." Henry didn't hear the rest.

The detectives were going out the door when he muttered, "Al tol' me to put the money in a safe deposit box, but he didn't say nothin' about signin' no forms."

The detectives stopped and Hines asked, "Al?"

Henry looked up.

"Al who?"

"I don't know," Henry said. "He didn't give me his last name."

They came back into the room.

"Where did you meet Al, Mr. Simon?"

"In Sparks, at the Nugget. We was sittin' next to each other in the keno parlor and we got to talkin'."

"And you told him about the money?"

"Yeah, I tol' him how I won it and came here to get away and he's the one tol' me to put it in the safe deposit box to get my room comped."

"And he told you to come here, to this hotel?"

"Yeah, he did."

"Mr. Simon," Hines asked, "Did Al have a bald head, baggy shorts, terrible legs?"

"He was bald and wearin' shorts," Henry said, "I didn't think his legs was so terr—do you know him?"

"Mr. Simon," Hines said, "it sounds like you were talking to Albert Collins, otherwise known as Al Colley, Alley the Egg—"

"The egg?"

"Because of the bald head?" Hines said, holding his hand over his own curly locks.

"Al waits around in casinos for someone to hit big and then he figures out a way to con them out of their money. He's worked Nevada from Laughlin to here and back. He's only been a con man up to now, but I guess he figured this was too good a score to split, and he killed his partner. See, he obviously sent you here because he had a man on the inside."

"So . . . so you know who did this?" Henry asked, hopefully. "You can catch him and get my money back?"

"We'll catch him eventually, Mr. Simon," Hines said, "but it's my bet the money will be gone by the time we do. I'm sorry."

Not as sorry as Henry was—not nearly as sorry!

Henry and the idiots were sitting in the bar in the Silver Legacy, having complimentary drinks. It was the least the management thought they could do. Henry was sitting between the two brothers.

"What are you gonna do, Henry?' Brother asked.

"I don't know what I'm gonna do, Brother," Henry said, "but I know what I'm not gonna do."

"What?"

"I ain't goin' back to Missouri."

"What about Mildred?"

"Maybe I'll go to Vegas and get a divorce."

"Why would you wanna do that, Henry?" Sonny asked.

Henry looked at idiot number two, as he sometimes thought of him. "Sonny, your sister is a terrible, horrible woman."

Sonny blinked and said, "So?"

"Shut up, Sonny," Brother said. "Henry, we gotta all go back."

"Why?" Henry asked.

"Because Milly tol' us if we don't come back with you and the money, not to come back at all."

"She told you that?"

"Yeah."

"Seems to me your decision is made for you, then," Henry said. "We don't have the money, do we?"

"Well . . . no."

"And I'm not goin' back."

"Whataya talkin' about?" Sonny asked.

"I'm sayin'," Henry replied, "that none of us have to go back."

"But . . . what would we do?" Brother asked.

"Find jobs, stay here," Henry said. "You boys are . . ." He groped for the right word. It wasn't "bright," and it sure wasn't "smart." Then he found it. " . . . big. You could get jobs as bouncers in one of the small casinos."

Sonny looked at Brother with a huge furrow in his brow.

"We could do that," Brother said.

"Huh?" Sonny asked.

"Well," Brother said, "Momma wasn't easy to live with, Sonny, and Mildred is just like her."

"B-but . . . what will she do?"

"She'll get along," Henry said, "believe me, she will."

Henry finished his drink and stood up.

"Look, boys, think it over. I'll be around for a few more days, decidin' what I want to do."

"We ain't got no money, Henry," Brother said.

"This hotel is lettin' me stay another week on them," Henry said, "and they asked me what else they can do for me. I'll get you boys a room for the same amount of time. That oughtta give you enough time to make up your minds. And you can cash in your tickets. That'll give you a few bucks."

"What do we tell Mildred?" Sonny asked.

"Don't tell her nothin'," Henry said, "until you've made up your minds."

"Where you goin'?" Brother asked.

"For a walk," he said. "I'll arrange for your room and meet you here in an hour."

He left the two idiots there, arguing with each other. Brother wanted to stay; Sonny wanted to go back. Maybe they'd split up, or maybe Brother would make the decision, since he was the oldest. But they had no reason to try to drag him back, even if they decided to return.

He started for the front door, feeling his pockets to see how much money he had left. He found a fifty dollar bill in his jacket pocket, and his last keno ticket, which he hadn't checked. He also had his Harrah's Pick 6 ticket.

He turned and went back to the keno parlor. They had played many games since his last one, so he just gave the clerk the ticket and said, "Would you tell me if that's a winner or a loser?"

"Certainly, sir."

He fed it into a slot and the machine *whirred* and took it in, then spit it out.

"Loser?" he asked.

"No, sir," the clerk said, and as he did the amount of money the ticket was worth flashed in red numbers on the readout: $30,000.00.

"Is that right?" Henry asked, his heart racing.

"Yes, sir," the clerk said. "You hit all your numbers for thirty thousand. Nice one, sir. Congratulations. If you wait a moment, we'll get you paid off."

Henry couldn't believe it. Thirty grand and the idiots didn't know a thing about it. His luck had changed, after all. He fingered the Pick 6 ticket in his pocket and wished they'd hurry up and come pay him. He wanted to go over to Harrah's and see just how much his luck had *really* changed!

Lucky Eight

Judith Van Gieson

After a string of successful novels about her Albuquerque based lawyer, Neil Hamel, Judith Van Gieson is now writing novels about rare book expert Claire Reynier. The landscape is the same, however, and the most recent entry, *Land of Burning Heat* (Signet, 2003), is the fourth in the series. The setting is also the same for this story, and for her gaming aspect Judith has chosen the fairly recent phenomenon of Indian reservation casinos. However, she also manages to paint a fairly horrific picture of the life of a working writer that made me shudder.

For Max

Rana Dumaine was the pen name of a romantic suspense novelist. Every year she produced a book that got great reviews (the *New York Times* said she had a poet's flair for metaphor) but had mediocre sales. It was a struggle to make a living, although her latest advance had made it possible to make a down payment on a small house and reenter the middle class world she remembered from childhood. She worked even harder on that manuscript, hoping it would be the one to take her out of the midlist and onto the bestseller list. A month before it was due her small, independent publisher was purchased and swallowed up by a large European conglomerate. The independent's imprint vanished. Rana's editor disappeared. Her publicist would not return her phone calls. She was assigned an editor from the conglomerate who'd had no experience with romantic suspense.

Rana was three months late turning in the manuscript but that went with the territory—or so she thought. Four months after she turned it in, the manuscript was rejected on the grounds that it was late.

"The manuscript was late because I wanted to take the time to make it perfect," Rana said.

"Well, it's far from perfect," her new editor replied. "The plot is poorly conceived. The writing is tepid. The metaphors lack definition. There's no romance. There's no suspense. This manuscript would be unacceptable even if it had been delivered on time. As it is, it's too late for us to fit it into our spring schedule."

"Couldn't you fit it into another schedule?"

"No," the editor said.

Her agent told Rana that if she sold the book elsewhere she would have to pay back the advance she had already received, but he didn't think that would be an issue because her middling sales record made the book impossible to place elsewhere. Rana had spent all the money anyway on the down payment on her house. She'd been living on credit cards and optimism while she finished the book and waited for the money due on completion. It was a shameful way to treat an author, she thought, a person who gave voice to the unexpressed joys and sorrows of everyone else.

She was sitting at her desk facing a blank

computer screen, shuffling her bills, fantasizing about winning the lottery or hitting it big at a casino when she heard the sound of a basketball bouncing down her driveway. It was Eric, the eleven-year-old boy who lived next door. He had a backboard in his yard, and as soon as school ended the beat of his ball began. Rana was the only grownup in her working-class neighborhood who stayed home during the day, and Eric often stopped by to visit. He was quick, he was dedicated, but he was unlikely to even reach Rana's height of five foot eight and he walked with a limp. Eric had childhood arthritis and it had gnarled one knee and made that leg shorter than the other.

Rana saw his face peering through the glass in her back door. Eric wore sunshine yellow shorts and an LA Lakers muscle shirt with his hero Kobe Bryant's number, eight. He cradled a container of cookie dough in one arm and a basketball in the other.

"Hi," he said. "I'm selling cookie dough for the school."

"How much is it?" Rana asked.

"Ten dollars."

Too much for a container of cookie dough, but not nearly enough for a child as lovable as Eric. Besides the dough had M&M's in it and the money went to a good cause. Rana gave him a ten, possibly even her last ten.

"Are you working?" Eric asked. He spun the basketball around in his fingers before giving it an alluring bounce.

"No."

"Wanna come down to the school and play basketball with me?"

Why not? thought Rana. She could use the exercise and it beat wondering how she was going to pay her bills. They walked down the street to Eric's middle school and shot some hoops. While she watched Eric practice free throws, Rana remembered a cheer she'd learned in high school.

> *Up in the air, over the rim*
> *Come on, Eric, put it in.*

The ball swished through the net clean as a whistle or slick as a knife through butter or smooth as a shark through water. Even when she wasn't writing Rana couldn't stop thinking in metaphors. She and Eric agreed to play a game. The winner would be whoever got to twenty-five points first. Rana was a foot taller, but Eric had the moves. He dribbled the ball between her legs and caught it when it bounced out on the other side. Rana demonstrated the hook shot she'd perfected in high school when she was the tallest girl in her class. She was lighter on her feet then; she missed a couple of tries before her hook came back. Eric got to twenty-five points first, but only because at the last minute he sank a three pointer from the back of the court. Eric was proud of his victory. Rana gave him a high five.

"I'm going to be the next Kobe Bryant," he bragged.

"And I'm going to be the next Danielle Steel," Rana replied. "But first I have to find a new publisher."

Eric gave his ball a sad little bounce. "And first I have to get my leg fixed."

Rana knew that would require an operation Eric's parents could not afford. His father worked as an air-conditioning repairman. His mother cleaned houses. Neither of them was covered by health insurance. The odds of Eric ever having his operation were about as good as the odds of Rana ever getting published again and turning into a best-selling author.

She walked him home. When she got to her house she baked a batch of cookies and ate every one, picking out the M&M's and eating them first.

The next morning she was back at her desk staring at unopened mail and unpaid bills. She was two months behind on her electricity and the power company was threatening to shut it off. The water bill was overdue, and the phone, and the garbage pickup. She was close to maxing out on her credit cards, managing to keep up the payments by borrowing from one to pay down another. But the credit card companies kept offering her more cards with introductory offers of 0 percent interest. She was tempted but she dreaded getting any further into debt even at 0 percent interest for the first six months. She saved the offers just in case and the stack was now inches high.

Among the notices from Visa and MasterCard she found a lavender envelope addressed to her in purple ink. Rana opened it and read a letter from a fan who said she was eagerly awaiting her next book. It turned the recent rejection into an even more bitter pill; there would be no next book. Rana felt like her life was a swimming pool and she was sinking down, down, down into deep water. When her feet touched bottom she might find the strength to push herself back up or she might expire for lack of air. She was tempted to bake another batch of M&M cookies. But she rearranged her desk instead, adding new bills to the stack of unpaid bills and new credit card offers to the stack of previous credit card offers. Rana had had enough bad luck in her life to know that when it turned, it turned with a vengeance. The worst part was waiting to see how bad things got before she hit bottom.

She felt she had to get out of the house but the

one thing she'd come to expect when her life was turning to shit was that her car wouldn't run. Cars had a way of mimicking the moods of their owners. She'd put the last repair bill for her ten-year-old Honda on her Visa card. She went out to the garage, turning the key in the ignition with trepidation, and was relieved when the car started right up.

She drove to a park in the foothills and went for a walk. The air was clear, wildflowers were in bloom, the view was spectacular, but it didn't pull her out of her rotten mood. She felt like there was a giant shoe dangling above her head preparing to push her down to the bottom of the pool. She was mixing her metaphors, she knew, but in this trying time she was willing to cut herself some literary slack. After walking through the park for an hour she realized that being miserable surrounded by beauty was even worse than being miserable surrounded by bills. At least at home she had the cookie dough. She got in her car, turning the key anxiously, but once again the Honda started right up.

Rana drove across town and back to her house noticing as she pulled into the driveway that her roses needed trimming. She had all the time in the world to do it now. As she turned the corner at the rear of the house she saw immediately that the shoe that hadn't squashed her at

the park had turned into a boot that had
stomped her house.

"Son of a bitch," she swore.

Lying beneath her window frame were shards
of broken glass. The back door hung open. Rana
peered through the opening into her living
room. The entertainment center was empty; her
TV and VCR were gone. She got on her cell
phone and dialed 911.

"The police will be there soon. Don't enter the
house until they arrive," the dispatcher warned.

Rana sat in her car and waited an hour for the
cops to show up. During the time someone had
burglarized her house, someone else had robbed
a local bank. While she waited she sank deeper
into the bad mood pool.

The cops arrived finally in the form of a tall,
cynical guy with a mustache and a world-weary
woman with bleached blond hair who was the
same height as Rana but thicker around the
hips. The fabric of her uniform stretched tight
across her butt.

"Officer Boyle," the man said.

"Officer Cartright," the policewoman said.

"Rana Dumaine." Rana's pen name had become her official name.

"You oughta put bars on your windows in *this*
neighborhood," Officer Cartright advised.

Who is *she* to criticize *my* neighborhood?
thought Rana. What kind of a neighborhood

could a cop afford to live in? She liked her neighborhood; it was a place where people looked out for each other. She saw beauty and kindness behind the plain stucco working-class facades.

Officer Cartright told her to wait outside while the cops checked the premises. Rana could hear them laughing and joking as they walked through her house.

"All clear," Cartright called.

It was Rana's turn to look through the house and determine what was missing. The thief had been in every room. Her microwave and camera were gone. Her costume jewelry had been stolen, presumably stuffed into the pillow cases yanked off her bed. The closet doors and drawers to the bedside tables were open.

"The perp was looking for guns," Officer Cartright said. "Women usually keep their guns near their beds."

Now the thief knew she didn't have any guns. Rana wondered whether that would make her house less appealing or would it now be considered an easy mark? The thief had passed on a silver bowl in the living room, a silver hand mirror in the bedroom and the tequila in the kitchen cupboard, but when Rana got to her office she saw that her laptop had been taken. Her latest manuscript was on the hard drive and she hadn't backed it up yet. All she had was a hard copy. What difference does that make now that it has been rejected? she thought, sinking deeper into the emotional pool.

After they'd examined the house, Officer Cartright filled out a police report, asking Rana her name again and writing down her physical description.

"What is your occupation?" Cartright asked.

"I'm a writer," Rana said, debating whether she ought to be using the past tense, wondering if Officer Cartright could possibly have read one of her books.

The policewoman's yawn told Rana she didn't read books. "Can you itemize what was stolen and tell me what it's worth?"

Rana listed the missing items, trying as best she could to estimate their value.

"If you have the serial numbers, you can add them later," Cartright said.

"Do you think I'm likely to get any of this stuff back?" Rana asked.

The policewoman shrugged. "Petty thieves aren't the brightest people in the world and they screw up. I'd say it's possible we'll recover some of your stuff, but not probable. Do you have insurance?"

"Yes."

"The insurance company will want a copy of our report. If you notice later that anything else is missing, you can come down to the police station and add it to the report."

Rana wondered if she was implying that people with insurance were expected to pad their reports. If so, it was the only helpful thing either cop said. They got back in their cruiser and drove down the street, leaving Rana afraid to be alone in her house but equally afraid to leave it. She went to the cookie dough, sliced off a piece and ate it without even bothering to bake it first.

She looked up glass companies in the yellow pages and made a number of calls but could find no one willing to fix her broken window that afternoon. What was she supposed to do? she wondered. Guard the broken window all night? Time moves at a different pace for the depressed. Rana had no idea how long she'd been staring at the window when she was aroused from her stupor by the beat of a ball.

It was Eric in his lucky eight yellow Lakers uniform. He peered through the shattered window. "You were robbed?"

"Yes. Watch out for the broken glass."

"This would never happen to Kobe Bryant."

"Probably not," Rana agreed.

"Kobe Bryant has an alarm system and someone to watch his house when he is on the road. You need to get your window fixed."

"I called everywhere, but no one would come."

"My uncle Jack fixes windows. He'll come."

Eric went home to make the phone call and a half an hour later his uncle showed up with panes of glass balanced on the back of his truck. By nightfall the window was in place. Rana handed him a MasterCard, hoping she had enough credit left to cover it.

"Eric's a good kid," Uncle Jack said. "It's a shame about his leg. It's supposed to be old people like me who get arthritis, not eleven year olds. The operation he needs will cost fifty thousand bucks. The family can't afford it. He'll never be the next Kobe Bryant. When he grows up, he'll be lucky if he walks without a limp. Eric said you write novels."

"I used to," Rana replied.

"I guess you can make dreams come true in books." He shrugged. "But it doesn't happen in real life."

"Well, you did get my window fixed before dark and I appreciate that."

"Happy to help," Uncle Jack said.

In the morning Rana called her insurance company. They said they would replace the stolen items with comparable new items or would give her replacement value in cash minus a depreciation of 25 percent. Rana had sixty days to make up her mind. She went through the list of stolen items to see what she could live without. The microwave, the VCR, the camera, the jewelry, were all dispensable. She could read in the evening and get by without a TV. The big question was the computer. She wouldn't need that either if she didn't write any more. She decided to take the sixty days' decision time on the computer and cash for the rest. It gave her enough money to live on for another month.

But what was she going to do after that? Rana had a proposal for an occult thriller in her file that she had never shown to anyone. She shipped it off to her agent and waited anxiously for a reply. She knew there was trouble when her agent answered with a letter. Her agent only wrote letters when the news was bad. The proposal was boring, he said. Written under a different pseudonym it would be unsaleable. Published under the name Rana Dumaine it would ruin her career.

"What career?" Rana thought.

She sliced off a piece of cookie dough with a couple of M&M's inside and took it to her desk. She had no day job to fall back on, having supported herself (more or less) as a writer for ten years. The only skills she had were that she could type and she could imagine. Seeing the stack of low interest rate credit card offers made Rana think she should add them to the police report.

She drove downtown to the police station and waited twenty minutes for her turn.

"Busy day?" she asked the guy hiding behind the bulletproof shield.

"It's always busy here," he replied.

When she read the police report Rana was infuriated to see that Officer Cartright had described her as a middle aged Caucasian female with gray hair and blue eyes standing five feet six and weighing 175 pounds.

"That's not right," she complained. "I may have a few gray highlights, but my hair is basically brown. I weigh one hundred and forty pounds and I am five feet eight inches. Officer Cartright might weigh one hundred and seventy-five pounds but I do not!"

The guy shrugged. "What is it you want to add?" he asked.

"Some letters offering me credit cards."

"Write that down," he said.

When she was done, he made her a copy of the report for the insurance company.

Rana took the replacement money for the computer and purchased a cheaper model. She began to look for a job she could do at home until she felt up to writing about romance again. After years of working in her nightgown and snacking all day, the thought of getting dressed in the morning and driving across town to work for someone else had no appeal. Over the Internet she found work typing handwritten mailing lists. Not a job for a creative person, but it was work. The only interesting part about it was imagining what the handwriting revealed about the signers. Since she would never meet them, she would never know. Typing paid some of the bills but not all. She was still borrowing from one credit card to pay down another.

The feeling continued that she had a shoe hanging over her head and it wasn't a basketball sneaker either. It was a heavy, hobnailed boot. The following month she opened an envelope from Platinum Visa. Were they offering her another low interest rate credit card? It wasn't an offer. It was a bill. A credit card in the name of Rana Dumaine had maxed out on cash advances in the amount of seventy-five hundred dollars.

Rana called Platinum Visa immediately and listened to several menus before she got a live person. "I was robbed recently and the thief could have stolen the offer you sent me and taken out credit in my name," she said.

"One moment please. I am going to transfer your call to our fraud department."

Rana waited, listening to relentlessly upbeat music that only increased her anxiety.

The woman who picked up next questioned Rana's veracity. "The bill came to the correct address, didn't it?"

"The thieves knew my address. They robbed my house."

"Is this your social security number?" The woman rattled off a number that Rana recognized as her own.

"Yes. The thief must have gotten it from something in my house—a bank statement, maybe, or a mortgage notice."

"Did you report the theft to the police?"

"Of course. In fact I went down there when I noticed the credit card offers and I added them to the police report."

"Could you send us a copy of the report?"

Rana was getting exasperated. "You're making me feel like I'm the crook."

"We're just trying to protect your interests, ma'am. We'll need to verify the theft."

"Could you send me a copy of the signature that was used to take out the card? I'm curious about this person who is impersonating me."

"I'll have to talk to my supervisor about that."

Rana returned to transcribing other people's addresses onto the computer. There might be a day when her creativity came back and she could resume writing fiction again, but she suspected she would have to touch bottom first. She doubted she'd gotten there yet; there had been a stack of credit card offers on her desk.

On Sunday afternoon as she sat at her desk

and watched the rain falling outside her window, she heard a knock at the door. She was surprised to see Eric. Usually his arrival was signaled by the sound of the bouncing ball.

"Where's your basketball?" she asked him.

"My leg hurts and you can't play basketball in the rain anyway," he said. He wasn't wearing his lucky eight Kobe Bryant Lakers uniform or cradling his basketball in his arm. His oversized jeans and sweatshirt made him seem tiny and frail. "But the Lakers are on TV." He brightened. "Want to watch it?"

"I don't have a TV."

"You don't have a TV?" Eric seemed incredulous to discover that there were terrible things in life besides being small and having a leg that ached in the rain. There was being too poor to own a TV.

"It was stolen. Remember?" Rana asked.

"Aren't you going to get another one?"

"I can't afford it."

"What do you do instead?"

"I read, and when I feel up to it I write."

"Oh," Eric replied. He came inside and sank into Rana's overstuffed sofa, poking the coffee table with his sneaker. "The only way I'm ever going to be the next Kobe Bryant is if I write it in a book."

Rana knew that writing was one way to make dreams come true, if only you could find a publisher who shared your vision. "Maybe you won't be the next Kobe Bryant," she said. "But you could study hard and be the very best Eric Marquez."

Uninspired by that thought, Eric sank further into the sofa.

"How about if I make a batch of cookies?" Rana asked, trying to cheer him up.

"You don't have to bake them," he said. "I like the dough the way it is."

"Me, too," Rana said.

She sliced off some dough and they ate it after picking out the M&M's. She traded her sunshine Laker yellows for his blue sky blues.

As the month marched on it became clear that someone had taken advantage of numerous credit card offers. Eight thousand dollars from MasterCard, sixty-five hundred dollars from First USA, seventy-five hundred dollars from Advantage Platinum Edge Visa, twelve thousand dollars from AT&T Universal, seven thousand dollars from Chase, nine thousand dollars from QWest. By the time the end of the month arrived, one hundred thousand dollars in cash advances had been taken out in the name of Rana Dumaine. She had to deal with one annoyingly officious credit card employee after another. At least she was able to persuade

MasterCard to send her a copy of the fraudulent signature.

It was intriguing for Rana to see her name signed in a script that bore little resemblance to her own. At book signings she used to embellish the *R* and the *D*, but basically her signature ran along like an electrocardiogram of a comatose patient. This signature was thick and bold, full of peaks and valleys. Every letter was firm, round and legible. The ornateness of the signature suggested that the fraud was the work of a woman.

Rana began to daydream about the conniving person who had entered her house and stolen her own rather bland identity. She wasn't a woman who sat around all day in a faded cotton nightgown eating M&M cookie dough and transcribing other people's names and addresses onto the computer. If she wrote fiction, no one would call it tepid. The thief had flair. Rana fantasized about what she would look like, wondering how tall she was, how much she weighed. She doubted her thief had gray hair.

She wondered what a perp would do with the money. Invest it in the stock market and lose 30 percent the first year? Put it in money market funds at 1.5 percent? Why not just spend it and when the money ran out perpetrate a new scam? There had to be plenty of other credit card offers out there, plenty of other houses to rob. The credit card companies took a hit for the cash advances, but if they didn't send out so many unsolicited offers, there would be far fewer hits. Besides, they passed their losses on in the form of higher fees to their customers. In a way Rana's theft was everybody's theft.

She felt better when no more bills arrived in the following month. She worked with Experian until she was sure her good credit had been restored. But she still had the sense that she hadn't touched bottom yet. The con artist waited just long enough for Rana to restore her good credit rating, then she struck again. Rana began to receive bills from local stores for things she never would have bought for herself: a TV with a forty-two inch screen, lingerie from Victoria's Secret. The bill from Victoria's Secret alone was seven hundred dollars. The bill from Ultimate Electronics came to forty-five hundred dollars.

Rana called the stores and received an education in true name fraud. All it took to establish instant credit in a store eager for the business was to present a photo ID (easy enough to fake), produce a social security number, and pass a credit check.

"Someone is pretending to be me," she told the man at Ultimate Electronics. "But she is not. She's a fraud."

"Can you prove it?"

"Of course."

Rana went down to the store taking her driver's license and the police report and showing them to the manager, a big guy with warm and sympathetic eyes.

"The con artist robbed my house and got hold of my social security number and other information that enabled her to pass herself off as me," Rana said.

The manager pulled out the fraudulent application and compared the signature to Rana's signature on the police report. The fraudulent signature was the same as the one that had appeared on the Visa application, round and bold, full of highs and lows, peaks and valleys.

"I'm sorry, ma'am," the manager said. "You can't trust nobody no more."

"Are you the one who took the application?"

"Yeah. It was me."

"Can you show me what she bought?"

"Sure." The manager walked her through the store, which pulsated with the beat of car stereos that were being tested by customers. The TV the imposter had purchased had a forty-two inch plasma EDTV monitor that came with a free progressive scan DVD player.

"Why did she want such a large TV? Who was she trying to impress?" Rana asked, struggling to make herself heard above the rap playing on the stereos. She avoided shopping at

Ultimate Electronics herself, feeling pummeled by the pounding music.

"She told me she liked to watch sports," the manager said.

"Really?" The only sport Rana had ever watched was figure skating. "What did the imposter look like? Do you remember?"

"She was about your height but blonder, maybe a little heavier."

"Did she have wide hips?"

"Kinda."

"I was robbed and the policewoman who came to my house fits that description. She knew my address. She had my social security number. Do the police ever shop in this store?"

"Sometimes," the manager admitted. "You really think a policewoman using a phony ID would be dumb enough to show her face in Ultimate Electronics?"

"They aren't the brightest people in the world," Rana said. "Sometimes they screw up."

She thought the manager was going to let the matter end right there, but he surprised her by showing compassion.

"Look," he said. "I'm gonna be honest with you. If you think a policewoman ripped you off, your best bet is to take whatever insurance money you can get, restore your credit rating and forget about it. The police are not going to prosecute one of their own. It's a jungle out there. You and I need whatever protection we can get, right?"

"Good advice," Rana said, knowing that a writer always has a means of getting even.

Once the perp had hit all the stores in town that offered easy credit, Rana felt they'd come to the end of their anxiety-ridden association. She doubted the perp would ever be caught. Rana tried to think of it as a learning experience, maybe even a source of inspiration for another book. She had learned a lot about human duplicity, but she was beginning to see light above the water in the pool. She was beginning to think she could write another book, only this one would not be a romance. Crime paid better, at least in fiction. She heard Eric's ball bounce down the driveway and was reminded that she had learned something about kindness, too.

She was waiting at the door before he even knocked. It was a warm, sunny day. The troubles were over and it could even be a lucky day. Eric was wearing his sunshine yellow Lakers uniform. It took courage to wear a muscle shirt when you had no muscles, to wear shorts and not even try to cover up a swollen knob of a knee. "Feeling lucky today?" she asked him.

"Luck enough to beat you," he said, giving the ball a competitive bounce.

"I wasn't thinking about basketball. I was thinking more about going to the casino."

"I can't go to the casino," Eric said. "I'm not old enough. You have to be twenty-one."

"I know, but if you're feeling really lucky, you can wait outside and I'll bet for you."

"You will?"

"Yup. What's your lucky number?" She asked, even though she knew that already; it was emblazoned on his chest.

"Kobe Bryant's eight."

"Let's do it," she said.

They lived in a city surrounded by Indian land and casinos. Rana rarely went. She knew that most gamblers were people who couldn't afford to lose, and she'd always considered being a writer more than enough of a gamble. Occasionally writers hit it big, but mostly their time and money got piddled away.

There was an elegant new casino on the north side of town and Rana took Eric there. The money the tribe made from gambling was spent sending their kids to the city's best private schools. Rana saw the tribe as reverse Robin Hoods who took the money from poor old people and gave it to poor young people. Still, it didn't hurt quite so much to lose your money when you knew it was going to a good cause. Education could always be considered a good cause.

"Wow," Eric said as they pulled into the driveway.

The building was impressive enough to make anyone believe his impossible dreams could come true. The view from the casino was spectacular. It was surrounded by mountains and sky. The entryway was framed by massive beams and stone walls. There was a fountain in front that sparkled in the sun in the daytime and under the bright lights at night.

"I want to see the fountain," Eric said.

Rana gave him a shiny penny and told him to toss it into the water for luck. She sat him down on a bench and said, "I won't be long. Wait here for me. Number eight?"

"Number eight," Eric said.

She gave him a high five and went into the casino. Even in the middle of a weekday afternoon the place was full of people sitting at the slots and punching the buttons like automatons. Many of them were retirees with plenty of free time in the afternoon. The casino resounded with bells, whistles and flashing lights. Rana walked up and down the aisles trying to find the right machine. There were three rows marked by the number eight. C-8 had digital machines that she didn't know how to play. D-8 paid big—$252,322.68 to be exact—but only took five dollar bets. E-8 was nickel machines. Rana noticed as she wandered through the casino that air around the five dollar machine smelled of expensive cigar smoke but the smoke was heaviest around the popular nickel machines.

Deciding to start there, she went to row E-8. Each slot machine had a flashing symbol that someone might find lucky, although they seemed more geared to the taste of retirees than to eleven-year-old boys. Rana saw a cluster of machines inspired by the TV show *Bewitched*. She saw others inspired by *The Munsters*, *American Bandstand* and Monopoly. She doubted Eric had ever heard of these diversions. Walking down the E-8 aisle, she looked for a machine with a symbol that would appeal to him.

She found a cougar she thought he would like, sat down in front of it and slid in a dollar bill. A row of buttons on the machine indicated she could play any number of lines. She picked eight, of course. On her very first try eight snarling cougars rolled into place on the screen. It was amazing. This could definitely be her and Eric's lucky day.

"Gamble?" The machine winked at her.

"Why not?" Rana answered.

Two cards came up on the screen and she had the choice of red or black. She punched red, which seemed like a luckier color than black. When given a choice, what kid would bet on black?

"Collect winnings?" a red button flashed.

"Yes." Rana punched the button, and a pile of nickels clanged into the metal basin. There was an empty casino cup on the floor and she filled it with the nickels. The cougar machine made her feel omnipotent and all powerful, as if she could make any old impossible dream come true. She wanted to run outside and tell Eric she was on a roll, but she might loose her place at the cougar machine. Besides all she had won so far was twelve dollars in nickels.

She slid another dollar into the slot, and punched eight lines again, but this time she got two howling coyotes, an eagle, three bears, a wolf, and a rattlesnake. She admired the wildlife but there wasn't a single cougar on the screen, and she had lost her dollar. That's how they suck you in, she thought, give you a sense of power in the beginning, take it away again at the end. She continued playing, winning a few, losing a few. Whenever she won, she got a high, even though she knew that overall she was barely breaking even.

She wished she had told Eric to bring his basketball. At least he could be dribbling the time away. She looked at her watch. Nearly an hour had passed. The smoke was thick at the nickel machines. Eric was waiting. Rana moved on to the five dollar machines in D-8.

During the time she had been playing the nickel machine, the payout on the five dollar machine had grown to $252,324.75. Rana watched the numbers roll up the screen then turned to a vacant machine that spoke to her.

"Diablo Diamond, ha, ha, ha, ha," it said.

She put in a five dollar bill and lost. Slid in another five and lost again. In no time at all she had lost thirty-five dollars.

"Ha, ha, ha, ha," Diablo Diamond laughed.

While she'd been losing, the payout grew to $252,325.02. The cigar smoke was making her gag.

She slid her eighth and last five dollar bill into the machine. "This one's for you, Eric," she said, and then she whispered, "Yes, yes, yes, yes!"; she'd found the way to help both Eric and herself.

Diablo Diamond stopped laughing, but the weary retirees in Rana's row continued puffing their cigars, and punching their buttons.

Rana went to the cashier's window and converted her winnings. She knew Eric would be good and bored by now, but the news she had would revive him.

He was still sitting on the bench, jiggling his restless basketball player's legs.

Rana gave him a high five. "We won," she said. "Big time. And it was your lucky number eight that did it."

"You mean Kobe's number eight."

"Whatever," Rana said.

"How much did we win?" Eric asked.

"Enough to pay for your knee operation or to put you through state college. I'll get a cashier's check and deposit it in an account for you." It was a stroke of luck that might seem incredible to some, but not to a boy aspiring to be the next Kobe Bryant.

"Wow!" he said.

"We'll have to discuss it with your parents, of course, but I'm curious. If it was your choice, which would you choose?"

"The operation," Eric said without a second's hesitation.

Rana wasn't surprised. She'd been to college and what kind of an example had she set? She lived in a frame-stucco house right next door to Eric's.

"Are you giving me all the money you won?" he asked.

"Well, your lucky number helped," Rana said. "But it was my idea and my effort, so I'm keeping half."

But half of what? The twelve dollars she'd converted from nickels to bills wouldn't do Eric any good, but one half of the one hundred thousand dollars hidden in her house would pay for his operation. That money would be converted into a cashier's check with Eric's name on it. *Winnings* wasn't the correct term. Some might call it fraud perpetrated by a desperate woman against her own pen name after a thief robbed her house and left the door to identity fraud open. But Rana herself preferred the term *bounty*. The losers in this gamble were the credit card companies. The winners were Eric Marquez and Rana Dumaine.

"That sounds fair," Eric said.

"It will help me to survive until my career gets going again. Money you get when you take a gamble is funny money," Rana said. "Some people might say dirty money or even smelly money. You have to find a way to wash it clean. Sometimes life steps on your head. Sometimes it hands you an opportunity at the same time that it steps on your head. When that happens you take advantage of it but, like Robin Hood, you should remember those in need and put the money to good use." She thought she'd mixed enough metaphors and given more than enough of a lecture for one day.

Eric agreed. "Can we go home now?" he asked. "I want to tell my mom and dad."

"Sure," Rana said. She knew his parents well enough to know they would accept her gift.

She gave Eric a hug when she dropped him off at his house, then she went to Hollywood Video and rented a bunch of classic crime films on DVD. That night she watched them on her forty-two inch plasma EDTV monitor. She looked forward to watching ice skating on the big screen in the winter.

In the morning she knew she was ready to return to work. She left her faded cotton nightgown in the drawer, dressed in a black Victoria's Secret negligee dripping with lace that made her feel slim, dangerous, exciting, creative, and clever, too. She'd already quit her job transcribing addresses. She sat down at her brand-new, top of the line laptop and under Roberta Wood, her own true name, she began to craft a novel of shifting identity full of crime, intrigue, deviousness and suspense, yet also full of kindness, sweetness and generosity, a novel with bad cops and good kids, that showed the worst of human nature and the best, a novel that was sure to find an eager publisher and become a megabestseller.

Sex and Bingo

Elaine Viets

Elaine is another author turning her attention to a second series character. After describing several of St. Louis journalist Francesca Vierling's cases she now writes about on-the-lam Helen Hawthorne. The first book in the Dead-End Job series is *Shop Till You Drop* (Signet, 2003). But you can get a glimpse of one of Helen's temporary jobs in this story, as Elaine illustrates that sex and bingo may mix, but the mix is murder.

It was a summer of sex and bingo.

Where Helen came from, bingo had nothing to do with sex. In her hometown of St. Louis, bingo was a game for women gamblers. They were serious and grayhaired. Stick cigars in their mouths, and they'd look like the men who played high-stakes poker.

But on a cruise ship, everything was different. Even bingo.

Serious bingo was silent as a church, except for the intoning of the numbers and the hallelujah cry of "Bingo!" Here bingo players chattered like flocks of parrots.

Real bingo players would sneer at these frivolous women who played one card. Serious players could handle ten or fifteen cards.

Only one thing was serious about cruise ship bingo: the money.

Twenty thousand dollars was the grand prize

on this cruise. That was more money than Helen made in a year. And Helen couldn't win a dime. She worked on the *Caribbean Wave*, and cruise-ship employees were not eligible for bingo prizes.

But Helen was sure there was a scam. She knew an employee had walked away with a ten-thousand-dollar bingo prize on the last cruise. This time, he was going to double his money and go for twenty grand.

She knew it, and she couldn't prove it. She was totally at sea, in all senses of the word.

Helen knew who to blame for that: her land-lady at the Coronado Tropic Apartments. Good old Margery Flax.

Seven weeks ago, Helen had been exhausted by the discouraging job of looking for work in Fort Lauderdale. One night, as Helen trudged back to her apartment, hot, sweaty, dejected and rejected, she was met by her landlady. Margery was wearing purple, as usual. Her purple shorts were spattered with red starbursts. Her red toe-nails were spattered with purple stars. Her pur-ple sandals ended in bows at the ankles. The Florida sun had turned Margery's face as wrin-kled and brown as an old lunch sack, but she had good legs and liked to show them off.

"How'd you like to get paid to go on a Caribbean cruise?" Margery had said. Her land-lady had on her best sweet old lady face. Helen was instantly suspicious. There was nothing sweet or old about Margery, even if she was seventy-six.

"I'd love it. I'd also like a million bucks, but there's no chance of that, either."

"But I can get you the cruise. My friend Jane Gilbert manages the fancy clothing boutique on the *Caribbean Wave* cruise ship. It's part of the Royal Wave cruise line, the best in the world. The service is superb. And the food ... What are you living on these days? Peanut butter?"

"Scrambled eggs. Ninety-nine cents a dozen," Helen said. "I get six meals out of a carton."

"And a cholesterol count in the stratosphere," Margery said. She was puffing on a Marlboro. "Listen, take the cruise and help out my friend. Jane broke her leg and won't be back in action for two months. Jobs on a cruise ship are hard to come by. Jane needs someone to take her job who won't take her job, if you know what I mean. I said you'd be perfect. You'll get room and board and make four hundred dollars a month. Cash." At the word "cash," Margery expelled a huge cloud of smoke. Helen waved it away.

Helen always worked for cash. It made her harder to trace.

"But Margery—" Helen said.

"And commission," Margery cut her off. "You'll get a commission, too. There are some high rollers on those cruise ships. When they win in the casino, they buy big." More smoke.

"But Margery, what will I do about my apartment here?"

"You won't have to pay any rent. My sister Cora's latest marriage just broke up. She wants to stay with me for a few months while she gets another face lift. I can put her up at your place."

Margery was still blowing smoke, but suddenly, it was all clear. Margery needed a place to put the much-divorced Cora, whom she usually called "my obnoxious sister, Cora." In fact, Helen thought Cora's first name was Obnoxious. Helen wouldn't have been surprised if Margery had tripped Jane and broken her leg, just so Helen would go to sea and leave her apartment for Cora.

Helen took the job. She had no choice. She needed the money.

She'd only been on board the *Caribbean Wave* two days when she realized she wasn't being paid to take a cruise. She was being paid to stand ten hours on a hard tile floor. After a day in the shop, her feet hurt, no matter how sensible her shoes. Helen wore support hose, but she could feel the spider veins breaking out on her legs. When the sea was rough, the merchandise swayed and danced on the hangers and Helen's stomach shifted and lurched. The walls seemed to close in on her. It was worse in her room. Her inside cabin was the size of a coffin but not as plush.

But Helen loved the sea. She could stare at the ocean for hours. Some days it was the green of old Chinese jade. Other times, it was a brilliant turquoise with dark purple patches. On rainy days it looked like wrinkled gray silk, and when it stormed the water swelled and roiled like it was on to boil.

Today was a turquoise day. It was also her day off. Helen sat in a deck chair with a fat paperback, alternately staring at the ocean and reading about a woman who murdered her unfaithful husband. Helen hoped she got away with it.

She still remembered how murderous she'd felt the day she'd come home from work early and found her husband Rob with their neighbor, Sandy. Rob had always claimed he didn't like Sandy, but he could have fooled Helen with that liplock. In fact, he had fooled her. That's why Helen picked up the crowbar and . . . Well, never mind. The crowbar made such a satisfying crunching sound. It was one reason why Helen had to leave St. Louis abruptly and change her name. She could no longer make six figures as an employee benefits director in a big corporation. She'd be too easy to find. Instead, Helen took a series of dead-end jobs that paid cash and kept her out of the computers. She rarely made more than $6.70 an hour. But if she had to do it all over again, she'd still do it all over again.

On a cruise ship, nobody cared that she was on the run. Everyone was running from something: old debts, old lovers, old lives. Nobody cared what she did, period. The seventies' hedonism wasn't dead. It had sailed away on the cruise ships. There were old drugs, new drugs, everything from pot to heroin and beyond. There was every combination of sex Helen could imagine and some she couldn't.

Helen enjoyed the free atmosphere, but she didn't indulge. Drugs made her muzzy-headed. Love made her stupid. She was still recovering from a romance gone wrong. She'd made yet another bad choice in men, and she didn't trust her judgment. For this cruise, she was a noncombatant in the war of the sexes.

Helen just wanted to read her book and stare at the ocean. Now a huge shadow blocked her view.

"What's a pretty little thing like you doing reading that great big book?" said a good old boy voice. Actually, it sounded like, "Wad's uh purdy lil thang lack yew . . ."

Helen gave the guy her patented St. Louis glare, which could singe the hide off a rhino. It had no effect on him. He sat down next to her. He was cute, if you liked men who liked dumb women. He looked like Tom Sawyer all grown up. His face was lean, tanned and freckled. His hair was silky blond. One curl hung down over his eye. Nice muscular body. Friendly smile that stopped at his mean, slitty eyes.

"Name's Jimmy," he said, extending a thick tanned hand highlighted with little golden hairs. "You're new. You work at the boutique. I'm the bar manager and bingo caller."

"I'm Helen," she said, leaving the hand dangling, untouched. "Even though I'm a woman, I can read and write."

"Aww, now, don't take offense. It's just that anybody with those long legs shouldn't be wasting her time cuddling up to a book."

"I like smart things," Helen said, sticking her nose back in her book. Even Jimmy should get that hint.

He did. "You know, pretty boxes kept on the shelf too long get so's nobody wants them anymore." His country boy smile brimmed with malice.

"Beat it," Helen said. "Before I report you for sexual harassment."

"Plenty of ladies are happy to be harassed by me."

"Can any of them read?"

"Don't need to. What I teach them makes 'em forget all about books." Jimmy grinned, but it stopped before it reached his eyes. Then he walked off.

The creep was gone. But Helen's ocean view was still blocked. This obstruction was much better. It was Derreck, the muscle-bound cabin steward. Derreck looked like a god. Unfortunately for the women, he was a Greek god. Derreck was gay.

"I see you met the ship's legendary ladies' man," he said.

"That's him? He's disgusting."

"The small-town ladies from Michigan and Minnesota love him."

"I'd rather be marooned on a desert isle."

"I guess I better warn you about the Italian waiters, too. They're very macho and great womanizers. Don't tick them off. The waiters control access to the passenger food. If you're ever hungry for a steak, the waiters can provide it, but you may have to provide something back."

"I lived on eggs for two months before I got this job," Helen said. "I can do without steak."

"I'm just trying to explain how a cruise ship works. Jimmy, as the bar manager, is an important person. His cabin has recessed speakers and other luxuries, all provided by thirsty staffers."

"Power I can understand. But I don't see how that slob scores with the women. Do you find him attractive?" Helen said.

"He's not my type," Derreck said, and shrugged.

"Is it true he has a new romance with a passenger every cruise and most are married?"

Derreck sighed. "Helen, Helen. You can take the girl out of the Midwest, but you can't take the Midwest out of the girl. Jimmy provides a public service. Our female passengers want a fling on their cruise. They also want it to be over when the cruise is over. They'll never see Jimmy again and he'll never see them. He gives them a nice guilt-free romance. You know, ships that pass in the night."

"One of those ships is going to hit an iceberg," she said.

"I doubt it. Jimmy excels at three shipboard activities: bartending, bingo-calling, and banging passengers. He's never made a mistake in ten years."

"There's always a first time."

"What time is the midnight buffet?" asked a chunky gentleman in a red shirt splashed with parrots and palm leaves. He was about sixty and looked like he was wearing a tropical disease.

"Twelve o'clock," Helen answered with a straight face.

The guy was buying the boutique's gaudiest cruisewear, so she was very respectful. Not only did she get a commission, she got the ugliest stock out of the shop. Mr. Shirt had won big at the blackjack tables and now he was showering his girlfriend with gifts.

"She's my little gold good-luck charm," he said, patting her round gold bottom. "I call her Lucky, and I plan to get Lucky all the time."

Lucky giggled.

The pint-sized blonde was definitely attracted to gold. Everything she chose shimmered and glittered, from the Gucci evening gown to the Armani jogging suit. Lucky was one of those women who looked like a knockout at first glance. She had a fabulous figure and blonde hair to her waist. On second glance, she wasn't quite so stunning. Despite the clever makeup, her eyes were small and squinty, as if she used a jeweler's loupe to estimate the value of everything. Her lips were thin and her long blonde hair was brassy and bristling with split ends. But she was built, no doubt about it.

Mr. Shirt kept patting her, as if to reassure himself she wouldn't disappear. Helen figured Lucky would stick with him as long as he had money.

"These platforms are cute. Do you have them in gold?" Lucky said. The shoe soles were the size of paving stones, but they looked sexy on her tiny feet. Helen noticed her toenails were painted gold.

"Let me check in the back." A quick glance

told Helen there were no platforms in the small stockroom.

"I'll go look in the big storage room down the hall," Helen said.

"No problem. There are lots of clothes to try on here." Lucky held a black-and-gold beaded crop top to her jutting chest. Mr. Shirt beamed as if she'd done something clever.

Helen unlocked the storage room and nearly dropped the keys in surprise. She hadn't seen Jimmy since their encounter on deck at the beginning of the cruise. Now she saw more of him than she wanted. Jimmy was wrapped around a slender brunette passenger. She was moaning and writhing under him. He was lowering her to a table bolted to the floor.

The woman's white linen skirt was hiked up and her long dark hair had tumbled loose from its seashell clip. She had a wide gold wedding band on her left hand. Jimmy's large red hands were working their way across the woman's bare back, like two crabs on a beach. They had nearly reached the string on her green halter top. The woman's face was turned away from the door, but Jimmy saw Helen and gave that flat-eyed grin. The woman didn't notice her.

Helen found the gold shoes and tiptoed out. She returned to the boutique a little rattled, and talked too much to cover her confusion.

"So," she said to Lucky, "do you ever use that luck for yourself? Do you gamble?"

"Nah, she plays bingo," said Mr. Shirt, answering for her.

"That's gambling." Lucky pouted.

"Bingo is an old lady's game," Mr. Shirt said.

"It is not! The last game of the cruise is at three this afternoon. It's a ten-thousand-dollar jackpot. So there. That's real money. You'll see just how lucky I am. Are you going to be there?" she asked Helen.

"You're wasting your time," Mr. Shirt said. "Blackjack is real gambling. Nobody with brains plays bingo."

If he hadn't said that, Helen might have skipped bingo. Now she felt it was a matter of sisterly solidarity.

"I can't play, but I'll watch," Helen said, thinking that described her life these days.

Helen missed lunch so she could take an hour for bingo. At two fifty-five, she put out the ON BREAK sign and went to the Sea Star Lounge. It was packed with bingo players.

Helen sat in the back, sipped coffee and talked with Trevor, the Bahamian bartender. Helen loved to listen to Trevor. He had the most beautiful accent.

Then Lucky flounced in, dressed in a tight gold-braided Escada pantsuit. She bought a bingo card and sat next to Helen. Jimmy got up on stage and told corny jokes like a third-rate comic: "You know why mice have such small balls?" Long pause. A wink and a grin. "Because they don't dance."

The women lapped it up like cats with a saucer of cream. Finally he said, "You all ready to win?"

At last, he was calling the numbers. "I-18. B-4."

Lucky squealed. "That's two. See. I am lucky."

She had a long way to go. The grand prize was for a cover-all, all twenty-four numbers on the card.

Helen watched, comparing this game to bingo back home. Helen learned the game at the old city bingo halls in St. Louis. Her Aunt Gertrude babysat her on Sunday afternoon. Gert was supposed to take Helen some place educational, like the zoo or the planetarium, but Gert and Helen were bored with them. Instead, Helen got an education in the bingo halls.

She learned to keep her mouth shut. If she said a word about their Sunday bingo games, she and Gert would really have to go to the zoo.

She learned to lie. Helen would come home babbling about the baby penguins or the star show until her parents tuned her out.

She learned that sometimes you had to take a risk. Gert lived mainly on her Social Security money. When she lost at bingo, she ate chicken necks until the next check. When her aunt won the five-hundred-dollar jackpot, she would have new slipcovers for the couch and filet mignon at Tony's, the best restaurant in St. Louis. She'd never get those on Social Security.

Helen learned that sin was more fun than virtue. Her mother made her eat sugar-free cereal and vegetables and drink her milk. Her well-padded aunt let her have hot dogs, greasy fries, a chunk of chocolate cake the size of Gert's purse and all the Coke she wanted.

Helen would sit and sip and watch. When she was seven, Gert got Helen her own bingo card. Helen attributed her number-crunching abilities to the reverent way the bingo callers said the numbers. B-6. G-54. N-43. You knew these numbers were important. They could change lives. They meant the difference between chicken necks and steak.

This cruise-ship game didn't seem like bingo to Helen. Bingo gamblers did not wear size-two Escada. Aunt Gert wore a JCPenney dress the size of a pup tent and smelled of Evening in Paris. She'd never touch the cute candy-colored bingo chips Lucky used to cover her numbers. Serious players like Aunt Gert used daubers, which were sort of like highlighter pens. Daubers were quicker than picking up little chips. Gert could handle fifteen cards per game.

Serious bingo players didn't say they were

lucky. They brought their own luck. Gert had an orange-haired troll, a St. Christopher medal and a plastic poodle lined up by her cards. She kept them in a purple velvet Crown Royal bag.

Serious players would never tolerate Jimmy, the jokey country-boy caller. Aunt Gert would have stomped out by now—or stomped Jimmy.

There were so many differences between cruise-ship bingo and real bingo, Helen couldn't keep track of them all. Her list was interrupted by Lucky's joyful shriek.

"O-66!" Jimmy called.

"Two more and I have bingo," Lucky said. "I hope someone else doesn't get it first."

"I doubt it," Helen said. "Jimmy's only called forty numbers."

Lucky looked at her curiously. "How do you know?" she said.

"I'm good with numbers and I played bingo every Sunday with my aunt. A cover-all for a small crowd like this will take at least fifty-five to fifty-nine numbers."

"Bingo!" shouted a woman.

"Yeah, you really know bingo," said Lucky sarcastically.

But Helen did know bingo. It was technically possible, but highly improbable, to have a cover-all winner when only forty numbers were called. That bingo was either a scam or a mistake.

She'd seen a scam once. It had caused a huge scandal at St. Philomena's church. An investigation showed the crooked bingo caller was splitting the pot with her best friend. The pastor was so disgusted, he banned bingo for a full year. Aunt Gert never went back. "Gambling is a matter of trust," she said. "When that's broken, it can't be fixed. Something is wrong there."

Something was wrong here, too.

A staffer who'd been holding up the back wall rushed to the winner's wildly waving hand. He began calling back the numbers. "And the last one is O-66," he said.

"That's it!" Jimmy said. "Congratulations, darling, you're the big winner. Step up here to get your jackpot prize of ten thousand dollars."

"Who won the money?" Lucky said.

Helen could see a woman pushing her way through the crowd to the stage. The winner had dark hair caught up in a seashell clip, a white linen skirt, a green halter top and a gold wedding ring.

It was the woman who'd been in the storeroom with Jimmy.

"It's a scam," Helen said to Derreck that night. "Sure as I'm sitting here."

They were drinking in the crew bar above the rope deck, which was really the poop deck. Royal Wave ships did not use the word *poop*.

Crew bar prices were cheap and the ship's staff sailed on an ocean of booze, except for the ones in dry dock at the onboard AA meetings.

Derreck was drinking with Helen to avoid a different temptation. The hunky cabin steward was in a committed relationship with Jon, a graphic artist in Miami, and didn't want to flirt with the crew.

"Are you sure?" Derreck said. "You don't like Jimmy. And it is possible to win after forty numbers." His jutting jaw was cleft, like George of the Jungle's. The man was ridiculously, heart-stoppingly handsome.

"What's the possibility that his current squeeze would win?" Helen said.

Derreck widened his already big blue eyes. "Really? The little redhead on the Panorama Deck won ten thousand bucks?"

"What redhead?" Helen said. "This was a brunette."

"Then you got it wrong," Derreck said. "He picked up a redhead this cruise. A school teacher from Akron. Divorced, cute and a little naive, just the way Jimmy likes them."

"Oh, yeah? I caught him doing the wild thing with a married brunette, about an hour before the bingo game in the stockroom."

"Interesting," Derreck said, and took a thoughtful sip of his beer.

"I thought the crew couldn't fraternize with

the passengers," Helen said. "I sure got a lecture on that subject."

"Well, they can and they can't," Derreck said. "Technically, the staff is forbidden. In reality, affairs by officers and uniformed staff like Jimmy are tolerated, but deckhands and belowstairs help would be instantly dismissed. It's sort of an upstairs-downstairs thing. You know, a Victorian lady could have a fling with her handsome footman, but heaven help her if she was caught with the bootblack.

"There is one unbreakable rule: No one on staff can take a passenger to his or her room. The cruise line put up cameras all over the crew sleeping areas to watch us. Cut the rape complaints way back."

"So where do the crew and passengers meet, besides my stockroom?" Helen said.

"Well, there are the lifeboats. We're always finding used condoms and wine bottles in the lifeboats. The top decks are another trysting place."

"I thought the security guards did rounds up there," Helen said.

"They do. Every thirty-five or forty minutes. They're easy to time. You just wait till the guard passes. Then you have at least half an hour."

"Are you speaking from personal experience?" Helen said.

"Not lately," Derreck said, and virtuously finished his beer.

"The crew has one more choice. In most ports there are fleabag hotels that rent rooms on an hourly basis. Want another wine?"

"No, thanks. How do you keep those flat abs when you drink beer?"

"Beer has food value. It's made of all natural ingredients, malt, grain and hops."

Derreck went for another beer. Helen stared out into the ocean's infinite emptiness. There was nothing, not even the lights of another ship. It did not make her feel lonely. She felt secure. No one could find her in this blackness.

Derreck returned with his beer and Helen returned to the subject of sex and bingo. "Why isn't the cruise director calling bingo? I thought that was his job."

"Because Jimmy's popular with the passengers and the cruise director is more interested in pleasing them than playing power games. Listen, even if Jimmy is guilty, how can you prove it?"

"I can't," Helen said. "Not this time. The cruise is nearly over. It was only seven days. We'll be back in Fort Lauderdale tomorrow. I'm going to watch him this next cruise."

"If he's crooked, that one is the big bait. It's twenty-one days, with twelve days at sea. Lots of sea days means more bingo games for the bored passengers and a big jackpot prize. Twenty thousand dollars."

Helen whistled. Aunt Gert would have thought she'd died and gone to heaven if she played bingo on a cruise ship with a prize that big. Gert had been dead for years, and Helen hoped she was playing bingo in some celestial hall with angel callers and golden daubers.

"Is there that much money in cruise-ship bingo?" she said.

"Gambling is big business on cruises," he said. "Along with bingo, there's Caribbean stud poker and the progressive slots. There's money in those, too, and cruise ships get a break the casinos don't. Casino jackpots have to keep going up each time the slots are played. Ships can roll the progressive slots back down after each voyage. Less of a payout. Casinos can't get away with that."

Derreck's second beer was almost gone, but he still had questions. "Here's what I don't get: How do you cheat at bingo? It's basically a lottery. Is he fixing the numbers or what?"

"I'm not sure," Helen said. "I think he's getting his ladies to work with him somehow. I have a theory he has two girlfriends, one for show and one on the QT. That's the one he's cheating with. But this is a different game of bingo than I'm used to. These players are not all that sophisticated. It would be easy to get things past them. It's not right. Will you help me nail him?"

"Might as well," Derreck said. "Now that I'm faithful to Jon, I have lots of time for a cheater."

How was Jimmy doing it? That was the question.

How did that bingo scam work at St. Philomena's all those years ago? She couldn't ask her long-dead aunt. Helen couldn't call anyone in her family. Only her sister knew where she was, and Kathy couldn't tell a bingo dauber from a mud dauber. Aunt Gert's illicit bingo excursions took place before she was born, but Kathy would have never participated. She was a straight arrow.

The twenty-one-day Ultimate Caribbean Adventure embarked from Fort Lauderdale and sailed the eastern and western Caribbean. Lucky and Mr. Shirt were replaced by other couples, some married, some not. There was the usual collection of single and divorced women, hoping for a shipboard romance, as well as older people enjoying the good meals and sea air.

The ship had barely reached Nassau, in the Bahamas, before Jimmy was flirting with a giggly little CPA who had a face like a china doll and thick, muscular, dancer's legs. The CPA, whose name was Emma, must have been very good with money. She was staying in an eight-thousand-dollar Royal Wave suite with two oceanview windows, a king-sized bed and a Jacuzzi. Jimmy courted her with free drinks and bottles of wine at dinner. She giggled at his corny jokes.

Derreck pointed her out to Helen. "That's Emma, Jimmy's pick this cruise."

"That's his show girl," Helen said. "If he's running the same scam as last time, then he'll have someone else stashed in the background."

"That's going to be the tough part," Derreck said. "Keeping the second one secret. A cruise ship is worse than a small town. We all know each other's business. Speaking of which, Lordes, the Vista Deck maid, told me that guy nobody wants to sit next to at meals because of his awful BO doesn't shower. He hasn't touched a bath towel since the cruise started and his shower is dry as a bone."

"Sometimes," Helen said, "you can have too much information."

Working in the boutique, Helen met most of the women onboard. She listened while they talked about their husbands, boyfriends and exes. The Royal Wave operated on a cashless card system, and that seemed to encourage spending. Helen was fascinated. Before she'd picked up that crowbar, she spent as carelessly as they did. But now that she was on the run, she'd grown used to living on minimum wage money. She'd learned to watch her pennies.

Nobody bought anything because they needed it. Men bought clothes for women to show off their own power. Neglected wives bought expensive outfits to punish their husbands. Women bought to celebrate a special occasion, get even with their man, or because they were on vacation and had to buy something. Emma the CPA spent lavishly, treating herself to delicate designs and light colors that flattered her china doll face.

Occasionally, someone would lose too much in the casino, and then the trophy buys would have to be returned. Helen dreaded those times. The loud silences, the unshed tears, the pulsating, palpable embarrassment nearly crowded her out of the room.

She listened carefully for the women to mention Jimmy, but they never did, not even Emma. He was a servant, part of the ship's fittings. She watched the storeroom like a cat watched a mousehole, but Jimmy never went near it.

He's too smart for that, Helen thought. He knows I know. He's found another hiding place. That would be easy. Cruise ships had more hiding places than the mountains of Afghanistan.

She followed him when he went ashore at San Juan, St. Thomas (which the crew called St. Toilet) and Georgetown on Grand Cayman Island.

He did all the things the other crew members did. He ate in little local restaurants away from the crowds. He stopped at American fast-food places because travel made you crave Big Macs and KFC, even if you rarely ate them at home. He drank in the bars and went for walks. Sometimes he took the giggly CPA with him, and sometimes he didn't.

"He's sticking with Emma. I've never caught him with another woman passenger," she complained to Derreck.

"Jimmy has become your great white whale," Derreck said. "You're following him like Captain Ahab." Derreck laughed when he said that, but Helen saw the concern in his eyes. Following Jimmy had become an obsession.

"Helen, why are you doing this? You know the cruise line won't reward you if you discover Jimmy's fraud," he said. "They don't appreciate having their eyes opened to unpleasant things."

She knew that. But she couldn't stop.

"I'm tracking him for women like Lucky, who didn't know they were being cheated," she said righteously. Derreck gave her the fish eye but said nothing else.

Helen knew in her secret heart that she hated Jimmy and she hated cheaters. Jimmy was one of the destroyers, the men who preyed on unhappy women and shaky marriages. She thought again of her husband Rob, who'd made such a fool of her with their neighbor Sandy. That's why she wanted Jimmy, and that's why she was going to get him.

At first Helen was afraid that Jimmy might realize she was following him. But soon she saw that when the cruise ships docked in these Caribbean ports, they flooded the little towns with tourists. Crew members met one another coming and going. If she ran into Jimmy on a side street, well, she was trying to escape the crowds just like he was. She nodded coldly and kept walking.

Helen met Derreck in the crew bar the night before they docked in Cozumel, Mexico. She'd made no progress. "I'm getting desperate. We only have two more ports."

"Something is going to happen," Derreck said. "Emma the CPA was giggling even more than usual."

Helen wanted to ask Derreck to go with her on the next shore trip, but he seemed distracted. He was suspiciously silent on the subject of Jon.

This time, Helen followed Emma off the ship instead of Jimmy. Some of the passengers went on the shore excursions. Others headed for the duty-free shops. Helen wondered how much Lalique, Royal Doulton and Waterford people could look at.

Emma stayed by herself. The CPA wandered through T-shirt shops and souvenir stands, getting farther and farther from the cruise-ship crowd. Helen lost track of Emma in a shop that sold onyx bookends and coconut carvings. Half a block later, she spotted Emma again, but she was no longer alone. She was hanging onto Jimmy like he was the last lifeboat on the *Titanic*.

The couple went to a dingy little hotel, blocks away from the bright new tourist hotels that lined the shore. It was painted turquoise, hence its name, La Turquesa. Helen was afraid they would see her. She was surrounded by swarms of grubby children selling souvenirs, begging for money, offering to show her the sights. Their older brothers tried to sell her drugs and themselves. But Jimmy and Emma were too wrapped up in each other to notice. Helen pushed her way through the begging crowds and went back to the ship. She didn't say anything about the tryst, but by the first dinner seating, the whole crew knew where Jimmy had spent the afternoon. It was amazing how gossip spread on the ship.

"I've read this all wrong," Helen told Derreck in the crew bar that night. "He's not carrying on with anyone but the CPA. The cruise is almost over. Tomorrow there's a stop in Progreso."

Derreck grunted a response. He was in no mood to talk, but he did listen.

"You could say I've been gambling, too. Progreso is my last chance. The day after is our last sea day and the jackpot bingo."

Progreso was anything but, in Helen's opinion. It was a dirty little port city. Emma, like most passengers, took the shore excursion to the Mayan ruins at Chichen Itza. Jimmy rode in the tender with the crew and walked around Progreso. Helen followed, thinking how strange land felt. She'd grown so used to the ship's movement she felt oddly flat-footed.

Jimmy stopped at a restaurant that had more flies and dogs than customers. Helen wasn't about to eat there. Instead, she went down the street to a pickup truck, where a man was lopping the tops off coconuts with a machete. She drank the sweet, warm coconut milk, then picked at the meat.

Finally, Jimmy came out of the restaurant talking to a tall, horsefaced blonde with elaborately curled hair. Helen recognized her from the cruise ship. She was Jackie, a beautician from Springfield, Missouri. She was married with two kids, she'd told Helen. Jackie must have scraped together every penny to take this trip with her girlfriend, Lila. They shared an inside stateroom on the lowest deck, a shoebox-sized room.

Jackie spent hours in Helen's boutique, looking at clothes she knew and Helen knew she could never afford. Eventually, she did buy a seashell hairclip. Jackie wore it today with what was obviously her best outfit, a peach dress with ruffles. She also wore a wedding ring.

Jimmy kissed Jackie. They walked up a steep rutted road, Jackie's highheeled sandals slipping on the rocks and potholes, to a hotel that looked like a noir movie set: a single bare bulb, a whirring fan on a sagging registration desk. The lobby was painted a vile yellow. Helen hoped the beautician thought it was romantic.

Jimmy signed the register and paid the clerk up front. Bingo! Helen thought. She was right.

She couldn't wait to tell Derreck what she'd seen, but she waited anyway. He wasn't himself that night when they met in the crew bar.

He hadn't heard from Jon in six days. His lover wasn't answering his letters, phone calls or E-mails. "Maybe he's out of town," Helen said. "Maybe his E-mail server is down."

Each excuse sounded lamer than the last and seemed to make Derreck drink more. Finally she gave up trying to make Derreck feel better before he was too trashed to help her at all. Besides, being sad only made him better-looking. He wouldn't be lonely for long. Helen was sure of that.

"You won't believe what I saw today," she said. Helen told him about the flyspecked restaurant and the fleabag hotel.

"There seems to be an insect theme here," Derreck said.

"There was only one reason you'd go to that hotel," she said.

"To collect cockroaches?"

"I've got Jimmy," she said. "The beautician is his accomplice."

"But what have you got?" Derreck said.

That was what she didn't know.

Helen was determined to be at the jackpot bingo game early, to watch every move. Derreck was there, too, and rather grumpy. There was still no word from Jon.

Helen scanned the audience. Emma, Jimmy's show girl, was sitting up front, flirting outrageously with him. She'd bought her bingo card when she walked in the door, waiting in a long line. The only reason Emma had a seat up front was Jimmy had saved it for her.

Jackie the beautician was a little more savvy. She'd bought her card when they went on sale that morning and avoided the rush. She sat in the back. Helen wondered if Jimmy wanted her there. Helen liked the seating arrangement. She could see the beautician's bingo card.

"Remember, it's a cover-all," Helen told Derreck. "The winner has to have all twenty-four numbers on the card. There shouldn't be a jackpot until fifty-five or sixty numbers are called. If the cover-all number drops below forty-seven, it's a scam."

"If he's cooking the numbers, why doesn't he just wait until fifty-five?" Derreck said.

"Because someone else could win, too, and they'd have to share the prize."

Jimmy had told his jokes, and the audience had oohed and ahhed over the grand prize of twenty thousand dollars. Finally, Jimmy started calling the numbers. The women were laughing and talking so loud, Helen could hardly hear the numbers.

"O-70. I-26. G-56."

She watched Jackie the beautician. She had covered all three of those numbers.

"I-30. B-1. O-69." Jackie had one of those numbers. Out of six called so far, she had four numbers.

Helen nudged Derreck. "Something's going on," she said. "Look how many she has already."

"How's she doing it?" Derreck said.

Helen didn't know. She stared at Jackie, but saw nothing out of the ordinary, except that she was covering her card at an amazing rate.

Helen looked at the stage and saw all the standard equipment: the bingo blower was shooting out the numbers. The display board lighted up when Jimmy placed a ball in the master board slot for that number.

"N-34," he called. The number went up on the display board, and Jackie covered yet another space.

"How many numbers have been called?" Derreck said. "Have you been keeping track?"

"Yes. Thirty-eight. It's going to happen soon. Jackie only needs two more."

"Three," corrected Derreck. "The center space on her card is empty."

"That's the free space," Helen said. "You're hopeless."

But she was, too. She stared at the stage. Jimmy was laughing, flirting and flapping around like a wounded crow. But something was off. Something was missing. She couldn't remember what it was. It nagged at her. She thought back to her bingo games with Aunt Gert. What was missing?

"O-63. N-36."

"Bingo!" Jackie screamed.

"Balls!" Derreck said.

"That's it," Helen cried, and sprinted for the stage. Suddenly, everything had fallen into place, and she knew what was wrong. She knocked Mrs. Edmond McGregor, sixty-one, off her motorized scooter, but Helen kept going, running as fast as she could.

Jimmy saw her charging through the audience and tried to pick up the balls he'd called, but Helen threw her body over the master board. Jimmy grabbed her and tried to pull her away. But Helen hung onto the master board and kicked him hard in the crotch. He fell to the floor.

"Arrrgh. My balls," screamed Jimmy. Helen wasn't sure if he was yelling about the bingo balls or something more personal and tender.

"My hip," howled Mrs. McGregor, the woman Helen had knocked off the motorized scooter.

"My money," screamed Jackie the beautician. "Where's my three thousand dollars?"

Three? The jackpot was twenty thousand dollars. Now the last piece of the puzzle was complete.

"You cheated on your husband. And you cheated on bingo," Helen said. The stage microphone picked up her voice and it rang forth from the speakers, the voice of an angry goddess. People were screaming in panic now and running from the room, knocking over chairs and tables, spilling drinks and bingo cards.

Jackie fell to the floor, weeping. "I just wanted a little fun," she said.

"Bingo is serious," Helen said, and her voice thundered through the room. Six security guards and the chief purser stormed through the doors. Bingo was serious indeed.

"So what happened after the purser and security showed up?" Derreck said.

They were in Helen's cabin. Her door was open to let the crew know everything was on the up-and-up, but the staff avoided her like a rabid lionfish. Only Derreck came to see her while she packed. She would be off the ship first thing tomorrow.

"I couldn't see anything," he complained. "The room was closed and locked and the rest of us were thrown out. Except for Mrs. McGregor, who went to the ship's hospital."

Helen winced and stuffed a pile of T-shirts into her suitcase. "I'm so sorry I flipped over her cart. How is that poor woman?"

"Alive and well and calling for her lawyer."

"Ouch," Helen said. Three pairs of shorts followed.

"What made you try a flying tackle on Jimmy?"

"I had to," she said. "If he got those bingo balls, I couldn't prove how he was cheating. I'd been staring at that stage. I knew something was missing. When you yelled 'Balls!' I realized what it was. Nobody was on stage verifying the numbers Jimmy called.

"That's the fastest way to have fraud. It's so easy on a cruise ship. The players don't know the game. In a shoreside bingo hall the other players would scream foul if someone wasn't called up from the audience to verify the bingo numbers as they're called. Even then, you can get collusion. It happened in a church bingo game when I was a kid. That's why many serious bingo halls have video surveillance with monitors the players can see. They wouldn't tolerate this lax security."

"But I still don't know how Jimmy did it," Derreck said.

Helen threw her tennis shoes on top the shorts. She wondered if the dirty soles would leave marks on her clean clothes, but she didn't care enough to rearrange her suitcase.

"First, he found an accomplice. He knew how to pick them. The women liked to cheat and some of them, like Jackie, didn't have much money. Three thousand dollars was a lot to them.

"Jimmy would find his mark, romance her, and then say, 'How would you like to win three thousand dollars?'"

"Three? The jackpot was twenty thousand," Derreck interrupted.

A pair of sandals followed the tennis shoes. "Jimmy couldn't help cheating any way he could. He couldn't even split the winnings with that poor woman, Jackie. He told her—and probably all the others—that he also had to split the take with a greedy housekeeper. Jackie believed him. The cruise line says there was no crooked housekeeper. Jimmy was taking that share, too."

"At the risk of repeating myself, let me ask again: how did he do it?" Derreck said.

"Cruise-ship bingo cards are sold ahead of time on the day of the game. He asked his accomplice, Jackie, to buy a card when they first went on sale that morning. Then Jimmy had her call him and read all her card numbers to him. He wasn't in his cabin, but Jackie left the message on his answering machine. He didn't even bother erasing the tape. The cruise line has him cold."

"He got lazy," Derreck said. "Jimmy's been working here for ten years. I wonder how long he's been scamming the cruise line?"

"He didn't say. In fact, he wasn't talking at all. But Jackie sure babbled. She was scared to death. I don't know which she was more afraid of—divorce or prosecution."

Helen found a pair of socks on the floor and crammed them into the suitcase.

"When Jackie called with her card numbers, Jimmy was in the lounge to verify the setup of the game. The stage staff, the grunt labor, did the actual physical installation of the bingo blower and display board. Jimmy stood around and supervised. He simply excused himself for a moment, went to a phone and retrieved the message with the bingo numbers Jackie had left for him."

"I still don't get it. How did he get the blower to put out the right numbers?" Derreck asked.

"He didn't," Helen said. "The ball would be B-5, but he'd call Jackie's number, B-12. Then he'd drop it in the B-12 slot on the master board and it would flash on the display board, because the system doesn't know the real number of the ball that's dropped in the slot. It just knows if a ball is there. Only the most sophisticated machines actually verify the ball is put in the correct slot, and cruise ships rarely have those.

"A bingo hall would have someone from the audience come up on stage and verify that the number was being accurately repeated, but most cruise ships don't. Jimmy conveniently forgot that step. And I couldn't remember it. My Aunt Gert would have never let him get away with it."

Helen found more socks in the drawer and stuffed them inside her tennis shoes.

"Jimmy would call out forty numbers or so before making his girlfriend the winner. Once the girlfriend called 'Bingo!' a second cruise staff person would go to her seat and call her numbers back.

"This person was not in on the scam. Jimmy, the caller onstage, confirmed the numbers and announced, 'That's a winner!' The winner was handed a bundle of cash—most of which she later handed back to Jimmy. But she was happy with her earnings. She knew it was more money than she would have made in an honest bingo game."

Helen made a final search of the tiny cabin. Her clothes for tomorrow were laid out on the single chair. She was ready to go.

"Jimmy was fired," she said. "He's confined to quarters until the cruise is over and banned from any Royal Wave ship for life. Do you think he will go to jail?"

"Not a chance," Derreck said. "The Royal Wave line does not want any bad publicity. I suspect Jimmy will retire in comfort with his ill-gotten gains."

"At least he won't be ruining any more shipboard bingo games," Helen said.

Derreck told her good night. Helen wished him good luck with Jon, but they both knew that romance was over. Helen suspected Derreck was relieved. Celibacy did not suit him.

Helen got a rather chilly thank you from the cruise line, and a not-so-gentle hint that she was no longer welcome as a boutique employee, even if it was a subcontracted position. But Jane Gilbert was tired of sitting around the house. Her broken leg had healed and she was happy to return early to her job on the cruise ship. She gave Helen a nice thousand-dollar bonus in commissions.

Helen's landlady, Margery Flax, was happy to

have an excuse to put her obnoxious sister Cora on the plane home a week early.

Helen's little apartment seemed big as a mansion after so many weeks in that cramped cabin. She enjoyed sleeping in her own bed. She dreamed of Aunt Gert and a piece of chocolate cake as big as a purse.

Jackie the beautician was allowed to catch the next plane back to Missouri. She was barred from Royal Wave cruises forever, but the cruise line did not prosecute her, nor did they tell her husband. She was happy, too.

No one got the twenty-thousand-dollar jackpot money. But someone did win the jackpot.

Mrs. Edmond McGregor, whose motorized scooter tipped over in the bingo debacle, settled out of court with the Royal Wave line for an undisclosed amount. It was rumored to be two hundred thousand dollars. Despite her unfortunate experience, she did take another cruise—on the QE II.

Breathe Deep

Donald E. Westlake

Like Lawrence Block, Don Westlake has seen it all, done it all in this business, and written about it all. Best known for his Dortmunder comic crime capers (*Money for Nothing*, Warner Books, 2003) as well as his hardboiled Parker series, which he pens as Richard Stark (*Breakout*, Warner Books, 2002), Westlake is as at home with the short story as he is with the novel. And since Jeff Abbott started us off in Las Vegas, we'll let Don Westlake finish us off on the Strip with a nifty little short short about a man taking his last gamble.

Black stitching over the left pocket of his white-silk shirt read CHUCK in cursive script. His pale, wiry arms were crossed below the name; his large Adam's apple moved arrhythmically above. Before him on the small lima-bean-shaped green table the 200 playing cards were fanned out, awaiting fresh players.

It was 3:30 in the morning and fewer than half the tables in the main casino were staffed. A noisy crowd at one crap table gave an illusion of liveliness, but only four of the seven blackjack dealers on duty had any action. Chuck had stood here at the ten-dollar-limit table for nearly an hour; it was looking as though he wouldn't deal a single round before his break.

"Hey, Chuck."

At the left extreme of the table stood a small old man in a COORS cap, smiling, hands in raincoat pockets. The raincoat hung open, showing a white shirt, a sloppily knotted, dark, thin tie and a bit of dark jacket. The old man had shaved recently but not well, and his gray eyes were red-rimmed and merry. The dealer saw not much hope here, but he said, "A game, sir?"

"Maybe in a while, Chuck," the old man said, and grinned as though he were thinking of some joke. "Did you know I came out of the hosptial just this morning?"

The dealer, his foot near the button that calls security, looked at the old man. He said, "Is that right, sir?"

"Sun City Hospital, right here in Las Vegas, Nevada. Fixed me up just fine. No more broken bones." That I-know-a-joke grin appeared again.

"Sir, if you're not interested in playing—"

"Oh, I *could* be, Chuck," the old man said. "I *might* be."

The night was slow, and the dealer's break was due in just a few minutes. So he didn't touch his foot to the button that calls security. "Take your time, sir," he said.

"That's all I've got," the old man said, but then he grinned again. "I love the big Strip hotels at night."

"You do, sir?"

"Oh, yeah. Oh, yeah. I hate Vegas, you know, but I love the hotels at night. I come in, I breathe deep, I'm a young man again. All the old words come back, run around inside my mind like squirrels. You know what I mean, Chuck?"

"Excitement," suggested the dealer, flat-voiced.

"Oh, sure. Oh, yes. By day, you know, I hang around downtown. You know those places. Big sign out front: PENNY SLOTS. FREE BREAKFAST. Penny slots." The old man made a laugh sound in his throat—heh heh—that turned into something like a cough.

"Sir," said the dealer, "I want to give you some friendly advice." He'd seen past the imperfectly shaved cheeks now, the frayed raincoat, the charity-service necktie. This was an old bum, a derelict, one of the many ancient, alcoholic, homeless, friendless, familyless husks the dry wind blows across the desert into the stone-and-neon baffle of Las Vegas. "You don't belong here, sir," he explained. "I'm doing you a favor. Security can get kind of rough, to discourage you from coming back."

"Oh, I know about that, Chuck!" the old man said, and this time he laughed outright. "I *belong* downtown, with those penny slots. Start all over again, Chuck! Build a stake on those slot machines down there, penny by penny, *penny by penny*, come back!"

"Sir, I'm telling you for your own good."

"Chuck, listen." Hands in raincoat pockets, the old man leaned closer over the table. "I want to tell you a quick story," he said, "and then I'll go. Then *we'll* go. OK?"

The dealer's eyes moved left and right. His shift boss was down by the active tables. His relief dealer was almost due. "Keep it short," he said.

"Oh, I will!" His hands almost came out of the raincoat pockets, then didn't. "Chuck," he said, "I *know* where I belong, but I just keep coming out to the Strip, late at night. It's a fatal attraction. You know what that is, Chuck?"

"I think so," the dealer said. He thought about showgirls.

"But what makes it, Chuck? Look around. No windows, no clocks, no day or night in here. But it's only at night. I *like* these places. That's when they make me feel . . . good. Now, why's that?"

"I wouldn't know, sir."

The old man said, "Well, I was in here one time, and a couple of security fellows took me out back by the loading dock to *discourage* me a little. There were all these tall green-metal cans there, like if you have bottled gas delivered to your house out in the country, and I bumped into them and fell off the loading dock and all these big green-metal cans rolled off and landed on me. And that's why I was in the hospital."

The dealer looked at him. "But here you are back again."

"It's the old fatal attraction, Chuck."

"You'd better get over it."

"Oh, I'm going to." Once again, the old man's hands almost came out of his raincoat pockets but didn't. "But I thought I'd tell somebody first about those green cans. Because, Chuck, here's the funny part. They had them in the hospital, too."

"Is that right?"

"That's right. 'What's that?' I asked the nurse. 'Oxygen,' she said. 'Any time you see a tall can like that, if it's green, you know it's oxygen. That's a safety measure on account of oxygen's so dangerous. You get that stuff near any knd of fire and the whole thing'll burn like fury.' Did you know that, Chuck? About green meaning oxygen?"

"No, I didn't."

"Well, what I kept thinking was: Why does a big Strip hotel need about fifty cans of oxygen? And then I remembered the big hotel fire on the Strip a couple years ago. Remember that one?"

"I do," the dealer said.

"It said in the papers there was a fireball crossed six hundred feet of main casino in seventeen seconds. That's *fast*, Chuck."

"I suppose it is."

"In there, in the hospital," the old man said, "I had this thought: What if, late at night, here in the casino, with no windows and no clocks, air-conditioning out of vents all over, what if . . .

Chuck, what if they add oxygen to the *air*? The very air we breathe, Chuck, this air all around us." The old man looked around. "Here in this spider's parlor."

"I wouldn't know anything about that," the dealer said, which was the absolute truth.

"Well, I wouldn't *know,* either, Chuck. But what if it's true? Spice up the air at night with extra oxygen, make the gamblers feel a little happier, a little more awake?"

"I'm going to have to call security now," the dealer said.

"Oh, I'm almost done, Chuck. You see, those penny slots downtown, they won't lead me back anywhere. I threw myself away, and I'm not coming back at all. I would have checked out of this rotten life two or three years ago, Chuck, if it hadn't been for this *fatal attraction*. Come out to the Strip late at night. Breathe deep. Get a little high on that extra oxygen, begin to *hope* again, get roughed up by security.'

"They don't do that with the oxygen."

"They don't? Well, Chuck, you may be right." The old man took his hands from his raincoat pockets. In his right hand, he held a can of lighter fluid; in his left, a kitchen match. "Let's see," he said and squirted a trail of lighter fluid onto the green felt of the table.

The dealer, wide-eyed, stomped down hard on the button. "Stop that!" he said.

The old man kept squirting lighter fluid, making dark puddles in the felt. "Security coming, Chuck?" he asked.

"Yes!"

"Good. I'd like them to travel with us," the old man said, and scraped the match along the edge of the table.

(continued from page iv)

MOST WANTED

A Lineup of Favorite Crime Stories

Edited by Robert J. Randisi

The line-up: Three *New York Times* bestselling authors, four Edgar Award winners, and other critically acclaimed past presidents of the Private Eye Writers of America.

THE DETECTIVES: The authors' most famous P.I.s.

THE STORIES: The authors' personal favorites.

Plus a special behind-the-crime-scene introduction to each author's creative process!

0-451-20692-4

Available wherever books are sold, or to order call: 1-800-788-6262